THE RETURN HOME

JEN TALTY

Jupiter Press

"Deadly Secrets is the best of romance and suspense in one hot read!" *NYT Bestselling Author Jennifer Probst*

"A charming setting and a steamy couple heat up the pages in an suspenseful story I couldn't put down!" *NY Times and USA today Bestselling Author Donna Grant*

"Jen Talty's books will grab your attention and pull you into a world of relatable characters, strong personalities, humor, and believable storylines. You'll laugh, you'll cry, and you'll rush to get the next book she releases!" Natalie Ann USA Today Bestselling Author

"I positively loved *In Two Weeks*, and highly recommend it. The writing is wonderful, the story is fantastic, and the characters will keep you coming back for more. I can't wait to get my hands on future installments of the NYS Troopers series." *Long and Short Reviews*

"*In Two Weeks* hooks the reader from page one. This is a fast paced story where the development of the romance grabs you emotionally and the suspense keeps you sitting on the edge of your chair. Great characters, great writing, and a believable plot that can be a warning to all of us." *Desiree Holt, USA Today Bestseller*

"*Dark Water* delivers an engaging portrait of wounded hearts as the memorable characters take you on a healing journey of love. A mysterious death brings danger and intrigue into the drama, while sultry passions brew into a believable plot that melts the reader's heart. Jen Talty pens an entertaining romance that grips the heart as the colorful and dangerous story unfolds into a chilling ending." *Night Owl Reviews*

"This is not the typical love story, nor is it the typical mystery. The characters are well rounded and interesting." *You Gotta Read Reviews*

"*Murder in Paradise Bay* is a fast-paced romantic thriller with plenty of twists and turns to keep you guessing until the end. You won't want to miss this one..." *USA Today bestselling author Janice Maynard*

THE RETURN HOME

AN AEGIS NETWORK NOVELLA

the SARICH BROTHERS series
book 4 of 5

Dylan's Story

JEN TALTY

WELCOME TO THE AEGIS NETWORK

The Aegis Network is the brainchild of former marines, Bain Asher and Decker Griggs. While serving their country, Bain and Decker were injured in a raid in an undisclosed area during an unsanctioned mission. Instead of twiddling their thumbs while on medical leave, they focused their frustration at being sidelined toward their pet project: a sophisticated Quantum Communication Network Satellite. When the devastating news came that neither man would be placed on active duty ever again, they sold their technology to the United States government and landed on a heaping pot of gold and funded their passion.

Saving lives.

The Aegis Network is an elite group of men and women, mostly ex-military, descending from all branches. They may have left the armed forces, but the armed forces didn't leave them. There's no limit to the type of missions they'll take, from kidnapping, protection detail, infiltrating enemy lines, and everything in between, no job is too big or small when lives are at stake.

As Marines, they vowed no man left behind.

As civilians, they will risk all to ensure the safety of their clients.

A NOTE FROM JEN TALTY

Some researchers have said there is a correlation between the ocean and being calm, happier, and more creative. Having spent a winter in Jupiter, Florida, I'd say these researchers are right on the money.

the SARICH BROTHERS series was born while I spent four months in Jupiter, walking the beach, visiting the Jupiter Lighthouse, driving around Jupiter Island, dining at various places on the water, and overall enjoying this next chapter in my life known as 'empty nest'.

The Sarich Brothers, while poor, had a good life, raised by loving parents. However, their father was killed in the line of duty when the oldest boy was just twenty and the youngest fourteen, changing their lives forever…

Each of the brothers struggle with a restlessness, in part caused by their father's death. They are strong, honorable, and loyal men. They aren't looking for a woman, as their jobs aren't necessarily conducive with long-term relationships. It's going to take an equally strong woman to rip down the Sarich Brothers defenses and help them settle their restlessness, so they can give their hearts.

The series does not need to be read in order, but the four novellas do follow a timeline.

Come join each of the Sarich boys in their journey to heal old wounds, mend broken hearts, and find their way to true happiness with the love of a good, strong woman.

I want to add that since this series has been released, and then re-released, my readers, have begged me to write Mrs. Sarich's story...well, it's coming! Look for Catherine's story, THE MATRIARCH, in 2020.

Sign up for Jen's Newsletter (https://dl.bookfunnel.com/rg8mx9lchy) *where she often gives away free books before publication.*

Join Jen's private Facebook group (https://www.facebook.com/groups/191706547909047/), where she posts exclusive excerpts and discusses all things murder and love!

Major, Dylan Sarich, knows only one thing: Delta Force. He has dedicated his life to the Army and his country and can't imagine doing anything else.

Until the unthinkable happens.

During a top-secret operation, Dylan is nearly sent home in a body bag with the rest of his team. With his wounds still fresh and on extended medical leave, Dylan returns to his hometown in Jupiter, Florida to heal his body. However no amount of physical therapy will destroy the demons lurking deep in Dylan's soul.

Dr. Kinsley Maren is an expert in PTSD and brain trauma. When her neighbor comes to her, begging for help with her son, Kinsley can't say no, especially when she meets Dylan. She's certain she can break through the anger and help restore his confidence and mend his broken heart. Only she never expected he'd steal hers.

For my daughter, Kelsey. You're going to make a great doctor!

wo things needed to be accomplished during Operation Stingray. First, find and rescue three Marines.

Second, make sure his men got out alive.

Mission failed.

On all accounts.

Major Dylan James Sarich closed his eyes tight, trying to erase the memories. But even if he could make the images disappear, he'd never be able to stop hearing his men, good men, scream while being tortured. The smell of burnt flesh lingered in his nostrils.

It had been four weeks since he'd woken up in a hospital in Germany, having no idea how he'd gotten there. Now he sat in the back of a small, private jet, donated by his oldest brother's in-laws, waiting for the cabin door to open.

He glanced out the window. His mother, three

brothers, and their families stood on the pavement. His niece, Abigail, helped her cousin, Kaylee, blow kisses while his nephew, Tyler, ran in circles around a stroller holding Michael, who looked to be passed out cold.

His mother held the newest addition to the Sarich family, Nick and Leandra's second son, Emmerson, only two months old.

Behind his family, a large crowd had gathered, waving American flags, holding signs, welcoming home a hero.

Some hero.

Nine soldiers' blood was on his hands. It didn't matter that the President of the United States had called him to thank him for his service. The president had even gone as far as to say that Dylan deserved a medal.

For what?

Surviving torture, while other men died?

Nothing to be proud of.

"Are you ready?" the Army nurse who accompanied him from Germany to the Palm Beach International Airport asked.

What was he going to say, no?

At least he'd be able to walk down the stairs. It would hurt like hell, but nowhere near as bad as being electrocuted. The skin on his chest tightened, and he swore he could still feel the current tear into his muscles.

Carefully, he pushed to a standing position, grimacing the entire time.

He took the hand the nurse offered and hobbled with his broken ankle still in a removable boot. The stitches that had covered much of his body, including the ones that curved down the side of his face, had been removed. The burns on his chest and back were healing nicely, according to the doctor.

His family understood the military and knew it would be weeks, maybe even months before they released a statement as to what really happened. His brothers, even when they saw his wounds, would refrain from asking him about any part of the mission.

Didn't matter if he could talk about it.

He didn't want to.

"You've got a lot of people out there happy to see you home," the nurse said.

"The town of Jupiter is a tight-knit community." He inhaled slowly so as not to shift his broken ribs, two of which had punctured a lung. "Let's get this over with." Standing on his own two feet still took more energy than he cared to admit. His back felt as though he'd been snapped in half. Every muscle shook and ached with each calculated step.

The pilot opened the door. "Thank you for your service." He pulled up his sleeve, showing off a Marine tattoo.

"Semper Fi." Dylan nodded, grateful to have been flown back by a brother, but shame filled his heart.

Three Marines and six members of Delta Force, dead.

They were the ones who should be given the hero's

welcome. Instead their wives, parents, children, and other loved ones buried what had been left.

The second Dylan's feet hit the stairs leading to the pavement below, the crowd erupted in cheers.

His mother handed the baby over to his brother Nick as she raced to the edge of the staircase where another nurse and a wheelchair awaited.

Hell no. If he could walk down these steps, he'd walk to the fucking limo.

All he could hope for was that he didn't fall.

'Hi, Mom." At six four, he towered over his mother, who wasn't short by any means at five-foot-seven.

"I want to squeeze you like a bug, but I'm afraid that will hurt."

He laughed. "A hug would be nice."

Holding his mother gently in his arms, he blinked his eyes closed. There were nine mothers who would never get to hug their boys again.

"Sir, let me help you," the nurse standing behind the wheelchair said.

"I'll be walking." Dylan draped his arm over his mother's shoulders. He'd been a teenager when his father had died and through it all, his mom had been the glue that held this family together.

He and his brothers had always been close and had all served in the military, but Dylan felt like the outcast. It wasn't just because he was the youngest, or that his career with Delta Force had been very different from his brothers and their time in the service. No. Dylan felt alone in a sea of marital bliss. He didn't begrudge any of his brothers their wives or children. He loved them all and couldn't imagine life without them anymore. However, that didn't mean he wanted that life.

"You were always the most stubborn," his mother said with her arm around his waist as they made their way across the tarmac.

His three brothers stepped forward and snapped to attention, saluting him. Tequila, his brother Ramey's wife, also saluted as she'd served in the Air Force.

"Uncle Dylan!" his nieces and nephews shouted, jumping up and down, waving frantically, their mothers holding them back from racing forward and attacking. It had been months since he'd last seen them all, and every single one of them looked different.

"I hope we aren't all staying at home," he whispered.

His mother laughed. "Just you and me. Mia's parents put up everyone else."

Logan's wife, Mia, came from boatloads of money, but you'd never know it by talking to her. She was one of the most down-to-earth women Dylan had ever met.

And she was perfect for his oldest brother.

"I won't be staying here long."

"You're on mandatory medical leave for two months, where the hell are you going to go?" His mother had never been one to mince words.

He let out a long breath, saying nothing. Hurting his mother's feelings wasn't something he wanted to do, but he didn't think he could stay with her for more than a week. He loved his mother too much to put her through the torment that raged inside his head.

"Baby Dyl," his brother Ramey said. "Welcome home."

"Thanks." Dylan wanted to look away. He couldn't stand to see the pain in his brother's eyes. He and Ramey had a special bond having both gone to West Point. Not to mention they had shared a room their entire lives.

"You look like shit," Nick said, sporting a forced grin.

Where Ramey had been the prankster of the family, Nick had been the most mature and never much liked Ramey's odd sense of humor. But over the last few years, Nick had loosened his reserve and that had been because of his wife, Leandra. She brought out the best in Nick.

"I look better than I feel," he admitted, slapping his brother on the back. Nick had suffered great losses in his life, but he managed to find love again.

Dylan couldn't love. Not that he'd really ever tried. Loving a woman just wasn't in his wheelhouse.

He kissed each of his sisters-in-law and their children, fighting the desire to hold them so tight he sucked the life right out of them.

"You must be exhausted," his oldest brother said while placing his arm around Dylan's waist, forcing him to lean on Logan's strength.

Logan had been a free spirit most of his life. Nothing much got under his skin. Then again, life had always come easy to Logan. Even when he lost an athletic scholarship, he managed to make it all work.

Dylan wanted to pull away. The idea he needed someone to lean on made him want to vomit, but truth be told, if he had to stand on his own accord any longer, he'd fall flat to the pavement.

"It has been a long few weeks," he said, heading toward one of the limos. He figured he could sleep for a week, and he might just do that. His mom had promised him peace and quiet. His brothers had only come for the night, to welcome him home.

And make sure he was actually in one piece.

Only he'd left a large piece of himself in an undisclosed location on a mission he couldn't talk about.

His brothers would return for the Fourth of July parade. The one Dylan hoped he would be able to get out of participating in.

"Can you manage dinner with everyone?" Logan asked.

"If I can get in a nap for about a half hour, sure. Actually, I'd like that," Dylan admitted. Being around family for short bursts between missions had always been something he looked forward to. He could get a dose of what family life was like for everyone else, and then go back to what he loved more than anything.

"Good." Logan held the limo door open. "We'll do something at Mia's parents' house and you can leave whenever you need to."

"Sounds good." Dylan had known Mia and her

family for most of his life. They were good people and treated him like family.

A sharp pain shot through his spine as he adjusted himself in the limo. His three brothers climbed in with him, closing the door.

"Mom's not coming with us?" Dylan glanced out the window. His mom helped the grandchildren into the other limo, before looking over her shoulder.

"She thought we'd all like some male bonding," Logan said.

"I've bonded enough with you idiots over the years," Dylan said, rubbing the back of his neck, knowing exactly where this conversation was headed.

The Aegis Network.

All his brothers had left the military and now worked for the special organization located in Orlando, Florida. No visit went without an invitation to come work with them, so why would this be any different?

"Mom is thinking about moving to Orlando," Nick said. Of all his brothers, Nick had always been the most serious.

And the most damaged.

Until he met his wife. He still sported a serious attitude, but he'd become a much happier man.

Dylan wasn't unhappy. Delta Force gave him purpose, and he loved what he did.

Well, he didn't love being captured and tortured, but everything else was pretty cool and rewarding.

"She should be with all of you living there." Dylan

stretched out his good leg. Well, the leg that hadn't been broken. Instead, he had twelve scars from where some asshole thought it would be fun to run a hot metal blade across his skin. "She could see her grandkids all the time."

"She comes down every weekend as it is," Ramey said. Talk about the least likely to get married and have kids. That was Ramey. Even more so than Dylan, or so everyone thought. "Puts everyone in one central location."

"Except you," Logan said.

The limo rolled through the gate. The sea of people that had gathered made room for the vehicle.

Dylan rolled down the window and waved as they passed through before getting on Interstate 95 for the twenty-eight-minute drive to his childhood home in Jupiter, Florida.

"I can make Orlando my only stop in Florida," he said, catching Logan's gaze.

"You're homeless." Logan shook his head.

"I've quarters in Ft. Bragg when I need them." If Dylan spent twenty nights there in a year, it would be a miracle.

"That's not a home," Nick interjected, glaring with those intense, deep-blue eyes. "Not to mention the possibility that your career could be over."

"I'm not even thirty yet. My career is far from over." Only, Dylan knew that wasn't true. Besides the damage to his body, his brain wasn't functioning properly. The neurologist told him the symptoms were most likely temporary, and he had been doing better, but only time would tell.

"I know what it's like to have an injury destroy your dreams." Logan leaned forward. In college, he'd lost his athletic scholarship and a chance to be a pitcher in the major leagues when a shoulder injury benched him for a season. "But you have other options and I've already talked to Bain Asher and Decker Griggs, and they'd welcome you to the Aegis Network family."

"The job is yours, if you want it," Nick said.

Dylan understood why his brothers thought he should consider the job offer. He'd be lying if he didn't get a little excited about working side by side with his brothers. The few ops they'd worked together on the side, had been some of the best times he'd ever had working.

But it wasn't Delta Force.

And he didn't have a wife or kids.

Nor did he want them.

"I appreciate it, but I plan on staying in the Army, with Delta Force."

"I want you to do me one favor," Logan said, leaning back and crossing his arms. "Take a month to recover, and then let's have this conversation again."

"I won't change my mind," Dylan said.

"Maybe not, but what happens when the Army pulls you from missions because your body can't handle it anymore?" Ramey asked.

"Or your brain injury isn't temporary," Nick said with an arched brow.

"I'm only a few weeks out from the blown mission. I'm on leave so I can heal, which I will. So let's not get into the doom and gloom, because I'm not dead and in a few weeks' time, I'll be able to kick all of your asses at once."

"Doubtful, baby Dyl," Ramey said with a chuckle.

"Call me baby Dyl again, and I'll ram this boot where the sun doesn't shine." Careful not to shift his shattered ankle, he lifted the foot that sported the boot, shoving it dangerously close to his brother's crown jewels.

"Hey, it's better than when what's-her-name called you baby dildo." Ramey grinned.

"Her name was Vicki, and she used the word big, not baby. It was not meant as a dig." Dylan's laugh cut short when the pain in his side reminded him of the steel beam that had crushed his chest.

The limo pulled into his childhood neighborhood, a trailer park on North Highway A1A on the Intracoastal Waterway, across the street from the beach. A few of the neighbors stood at the gate, and a big welcome home sign hung over his mother's double-wide that overlooked the water.

Logan opened the limo door, helping Dylan to his feet. "I'll send the limo back in about an hour."

The driver popped the trunk and set his rucksack on the front porch. Logan quickly opened the front door, taking the bag.

Dylan took the two steps slowly, gripping the cane, turning his knuckles white. He had a bottle full of pain pills but hadn't taken a single one. He didn't like how they made his mind fog over. If he was going to get through this, he needed to know what his body could really handle, and when.

He also needed to keep his mind as sharp as possible, and doping up would only make things worse.

"I put your bag in your old room, and Mom has the fridge fully stocked." Logan stood at the front door with his hands on his hips. "Do you want us to stay until dinner?"

"No. I told Mom I wanted to nap, so I appreciate you all giving me a little space."

Logan nodded and left, leaving Dylan alone with his thoughts.

He hobbled to the bookshelf and pulled down the picture of him, his brothers, and his father on the last day they'd seen their dad alive.

Stick together, boys. Make sure you always have each other's back.

A dryness rubbed across his eyes. "I miss you, Dad."

insley Maron watched as her neighbor's son sat on the front porch, nursing a beer, staring off at the water. A welcome home sign hung proudly over the porch and dozens of small American flags dotted the tiny front yard, swaying in the summer breeze. It was fitting since the Fourth of July was only a couple of weeks away.

The man checked his watch, then glanced in her direction. "Can I help you?" he asked with a clipped tone.

She supposed she deserved that for staring. "Sorry. I'm Kinsley. You must be Dylan."

"In the flesh." He raised his beer. "I take it you know my mother."

"And your brothers." She stood, taking her glass of wine, and made her way across the yard. No reason to yell, and her curiosity had gotten the better of her, considering her profession. As a therapist, specializing in PTSD and brain trauma, she'd seen her share of military men after combat.

Dylan's case, at least from what his mother had told her, appeared to be extreme, though she had not gone into details, only mentioned perhaps making a recommendation for her son to make an appointment with her at her office.

She stood at the bottom of the steps, feeling uneasy about the way Dylan eyed her. It wasn't sexual in nature, but it didn't seem friendly either.

"Are you the shrink my mother thinks I should talk to?"

Kinsley swallowed. Not out of fear, but the anger laced to every syllable struck her skin like fire. "I'm a psychiatrist."

"Well, you can tell my mother I'm just fine."

"I can't tell her that because I don't even know you, and for the record, I'm not soliciting business. You asked who I was, so I told you. I'm just trying to be neighborly. Your mother talks about you often." Now who spoke with a defensive attitude?

He grunted. "I'm sure she does. Either trying to marry me off or now get my head examined."

"Is your mom home?" Deciding Dylan didn't want to have anything to do with her, she opted to move on, and it seemed only appropriate to visit with his mother, or at the very least say hello.

"She's at the Vanderlin estate with the rest of my family."

"Logan's wife," Kinsley said softly. "I've never met Mia's folks, but I hear they are very nice."

"That they are." He stood, scrunching his face, but his eyes went wide, and he winced.

"What do you need? I'll go get it for you."

"I'm not an invalid," he said, glaring.

She stared back with narrowed eyes. "I never said you were, but why be in pain when someone is offering to help, or are you too prideful for that?"

Gripping the seat, he lowered himself into it. "Ouch."

"I really didn't mean to be rude."

"But I did, and if my mother knew that, she'd tug at my ear, and nothing hurts more than that." His finger and thumb rubbed his earlobe while he made a weird face. "If you wouldn't mind getting me another beer and grab one for yourself. Might as well join me until the limo comes back to take me to dinner."

"I'm good with my wine." She set her plastic glass on the table before entering Catherine Sarich's home. For the last few weeks, Kinsley spent hours in the evening listening to her neighbor express her concerns regarding her youngest son's hospital stay. Kinsley had been honest about what she knew about the injuries, more specifically, the brain trauma, but did her best to ease Catherine's mind.

Seeing Dylan face to face, Kinsley didn't know what to think. His closed-off demeanor emulated anger and sarcasm in a way she wouldn't expect from a Sarich. All the brothers could be described as broken souls in some way, but they managed to patch those wounds and build solid foundations with their families.

Dylan seemed to be a lost man with no sense of self, except for being the kind of man that would die for his brothers-in-arms.

She wondered if that was half his problem.

Kinsley popped open the beer before heading back out. The sun hovered over the Intracoastal as it descended in the sky.

"Thanks," he said as he took the beer and brought it to his lips. A raised cut that had yet to finish healing lined the side of his face. All his mother had been told was that Dylan and his team had been in hand-to-hand combat with the enemy and lost. The mission, though failed, was classified, even her father couldn't get her the information and he was friends with some high-ranking generals.

She sat in the chair he offered, trying to ignore the tickle of guilt for trying to find out any information about Dylan, or what had happened to him.

It was none of her business, and she didn't think it would be a good idea to take him on as a client, no matter how fascinated she was with his case.

"I'm sure you don't need a lecture from me on alcohol and—"

"I'm not taking any pain killers, this is my second beer, and I don't know what my mother is filling your head with, but when I left the hospital in Germany, they ran a bunch of tests, and my cognitive abilities are much better, and they suspect I will fully recover." He raised the glass longneck and swigged as if to prove a point.

"*For the record*, your mom didn't fill my mind with anything other than asking me for some medical clarifications on the information she and your brothers were given from the doctors in Germany." She stood, taking her half-empty glass of wine. "If there is anything I can do for you, don't hesitate to ask."

"Wait," he said, letting out a long breath. "I'm sorry. I'm being an asshole, and you don't deserve that. Please, sit and hang out with me while I wait for my ride." He glanced at his watch. "Let me make up for my bad behavior, please?"

Who was she to ignore a perfectly good apology? "I don't really think your behavior is all that bad considering I invaded your space without an invitation."

He let out a chuckle. It had a nice, throaty timbre, sending a warm wave across her skin. Even though he had a darkness in his deep-sapphire eyes, hidden somewhere behind them, she could sense a lightness begging to come out.

"To be totally honest, my mother has sent me three text messages about how I should go introduce myself to you, and she makes me nuts constantly trying to fix me up."

"I can understand that, but if it makes you feel any better, she hasn't said anything to me about dating you." She set her wine on the table.

He dropped his chin to his chest, arching a brow. "That, I don't believe."

"Oh, she might have shown me a picture or two of you when I first moved in, but obviously her focus changed when you were injured."

He set his beer on the table and shifted, taking in a short, raspy breath. "My mother means well, this I know with all my heart, but really, I'm happy with my life, and I'm recovering well."

She didn't know if he was trying to sell her, or himself, but she'd let that part of the conversation end there.

"So, how long are you in town for?"

"Not sure," he said, turning his head back toward the water. "I'm supposed to be the center of attention at the Fourth of July parade."

"That's in two weeks."

"This will be the longest visit I've had since my very first deployment."

"Enjoy it and let your mother spoil you. Before you know it, you'll be back doing whatever it is you do for the military."

He dropped his head back. "I hope so. My career is my life."

No sooner did she open her mouth than a limo rolled around the corner.

The rear passenger side opened, and Ramey stepped from the vehicle.

"Hey, Kinsley. I see you met the youngest brother, Baby Dyl."

"Watch it, bro, I'll kick your ass if you keep calling me that." Dylan stood, gripping his cane.

She resisted the urge to rush to his side. After only spending a short time with him, she knew his pride would get in the way of allowing her to assist him physically.

"I best be on my way." She picked up her wine glass. "It was nice to meet you, Dylan." She nodded as she headed down the steps. "Good to see you again, Ramey. Say hello to your beautiful bride and all your spunky little girls."

"We'll all be back for the parade. I hope you'll join us."

"I will probably do that," she said as she strolled back to her front porch, glancing over her shoulder. "If I don't, I fear your mother will give me her evil eye."

"That isn't anywhere near as bad as the ear tug." Dylan hobbled down the steps, his face scrunched in pain. "Thanks for joining me for a drink."

She stood on the edge of the steps to her trailer and watched as the sexy, broken man slid into the limo. Letting out a long, slow breath, she tried to ignore the pull Dylan had. She told herself the desire to get to know him was simply a hazard of her job.

Not any kind of attraction.

―――――

*D*ylan eased himself back in the luxurious sofa in the Vanderlins' vast family room that had to be the size of his mother's double-wide. He let out a long breath, wondering why he felt so bitter all of a sudden. He never went without as a kid. Sure, his parents didn't buy him a brand-new car the day he turned sixteen, but they did teach him the value of a dollar, the importance of a good work ethic, and how to stand on his own two feet.

The Vanderlins had done the same, they just could also give their kids their own pool, a view of the Intracoastal and the ocean, along with fancy schools.

Well, fuck, Dylan had gone to West Point. That was quite the accomplishment, and Mia and her family weren't a bunch of rich assholes who treated those with less like they were beneath them. They were good people who didn't deserve Dylan's foul mood.

"Let's get all these munchkins in the tub," Dylan's mother said as she chased down Kayla, Ramey's daughter, who had the energy of the sun and tenacity of a lion protecting her cubs. The kid had no fear and a giant-size confidence in a pint-size body.

"Grandma. Get me!" Tyler, Nick's oldest, exclaimed as he tried to catch up, but to no avail. While he also had boatloads of energy, he had a timid side to him and a soft heart, which was going to get him in trouble with the ladies.

"Do I have to take a bath with them?" Abigail said, clinging to Logan's pant leg. "Can't I have a shower? I'm a big girl now. Not a baby."

Dylan bit back a smile. Nothing like listening to children try to reason with their parents.

"I'm no baby," Kayla said, stopping dead in her

tracks in the middle of the open family room, swiping her blond curls from her face.

"You're my baby girl," Ramey said from his spot on the floor.

Kayla rolled her eyes, pushing out a long breath.

"You're so in trouble with that one. The female version of Ramey," Dylan said with a laugh.

"But better-looking like her mama," Ramey said, reaching out and grabbing Kayla, tossing her to the floor and tickling her belly while she giggled.

"Daddy!" Abigail fisted her little hand and sent it crashing into his shin. "I want to take a shower."

"You love Nana's big tub. Now go with Grandma. Nana is setting up the big television in Mommy and Daddy's room for you all to watch Nemo," Logan said.

"Fine," Abigail said, pointing her little, pudgy finger up at her father. "But only if I get popcorn."

Dylan put his hand over his mouth, trying to wipe the smile off his face, but damn it felt good to feel light-hearted about something.

"Don't talk sass to your father, young lady," Mia said, coming in from the kitchen and scooping the little girl up in her arms. "I'll help your mom." Mia kissed Logan on the cheek. "Tequila and Leandra have the two babies upstairs. We'll leave you boys to catch up."

Nick waltzed in with a bottle of wine and four glasses. He held them up in the air. "I think this family has turned me into a wine snob."

Logan took the glasses, setting them on the coffee table. "You know, that bottle doesn't cost more than thirty dollars. My father-in-law has an entire cellar full of inexpensive wine and that's his favorite."

"I don't think I ever even tried wine until you and Mia got back together." Nick plopped himself on the sofa. "And now I think I prefer it over beer half the time."

"It's called being a mature grown-up," Dylan said before he burst out laughing, then coughing as he clutched at his side. "Shit," he muttered. "That fucking hurts." He breathed slowly and not very deeply. The last x-ray showed his ribs were close to being healed, but not close enough.

"You okay?" Nick rested his arm on Dylan's shoulder.

Ramey and Logan had both moved closer, sitting on the floor in front of the coffee table.

"Do I look like I'm okay?"

"You're a bigger baby than any one of those toddlers," Ramey said in a teasing tone. "Every time you got hurt as a kid, you'd bawl like a little girl."

"That's funny coming from you since when you *thought* you broke your arm, you screamed like a dying cow, and it was only a sprain." Logan finished pouring the wine, making sure the glasses were filled and the bottle empty. "Here's to one for all, and all for one."

Dylan clinked his glass with each of his brothers. "I've got your back."

His brothers repeated the mantra. A deafening silence filled the room. Dylan sipped his wine, his thoughts going back to his father. Images of his childhood flashed across his mind. Running and playing in the street with his brothers. His father and Logan teaching him how to swing a baseball bat. His father and Nick teaching him how to shoot a gun. And he and Ramey building a picnic table for their neighbors under the watchful eyes of their father.

But it always came back to their last fishing trip.

The last time his brothers had seen their father alive.

The next day, Dylan watched his father take his last breath.

Logan swirled his glass. "Dad hated wine."

"But he drank it for Mom," Nick said. "Every anniversary and every birthday, he'd bring her a bottle."

"And daisies," Dylan added.

"He'd harass the hell out of us for actually enjoying this bottle." Ramey took a big swig. He enjoyed wine, but he drank it like he was doing shots. "I can hear him say, *'ya'll are a bunch of wusses. Real men drink Crown.'*"

"God, I hate that stuff." Logan shook his head. "I remember right before I went off to college, Dad gave me a shot. I thought I was going to puke right there."

"I've got news for you," their mother said, waltzing into the room with another bottle and a glass for herself. "He hated that shit too."

"Such language, Mom. Really. My poor innocent ears." Ramey held out his glass, while his mother went about filling everyone's before snuggling on the sofa between Nick and Dylan.

"Ramey, you're about as innocent as Logan is funny." His mother patted Nick's leg.

"Hey. Thanks a lot, Mom," Nick said.

"If he hated it so much, why did he drink it?" Logan asked, rubbing his chin. "I just always remember there was a bottle in the house, and oh boy, when Grandpa came to visit, they'd stay up drinking that swill all night."

"That's where you're wrong. His father loved that stuff, and it was just your dad trying to bond with him. Your dad pretty much only liked his beer."

"You're joking," Dylan said, staring at his mother with his jaw gaping open. They spoke of their father often when they were all together, but their mother rarely gave up any stories other than the usual tales.

"Nope." His mother shook her head. "So, when your grandpa died, your father decided he should at least continue with the tradition and tried to get Logan to drink that crap."

"He gave me and Joanne a bottle of it on our wedding day," Nick said. There had been a time when Nick couldn't even utter his late wife's name.

Dylan tapped his chest, his heart beating faster. He loved his family. Loved being with his brothers, but as always, shortly after he arrived, he began counting the moments until his next deployment.

Only this time, he didn't know when that would be.

"He wanted to carry on what his father had started."

"I read Tyler *The Little Engine That Could* every

chance I get," Nick said with a sigh. "Dad loved that story."

"That he did. Almost as much as he did fishing." His mother finished her drink and stood. "It's nice to have all my boys in one place again."

"It's good to be home." Dylan reached up and took his mother's hand and kissed it. "I mean that."

"I know you do. I also know the second you get the thumbs up, you'll be in the back of a C-130 transport plane on to your next assignment." She bent over and pressed her lips on his forehead. "But until then, I'm going to have my boys together as much as I can."

---

he darkness of night seeped into Dylan's bones the day his father had died. Ever since then, Dylan felt a restlessness every time his head hit the pillow. Years of training, first with the Army, then with Delta Force, gave him the strength to fend off the nightmares.

Until now.

This wasn't his first failed mission. Nor was it the first one where good men had died. But it was the first time Dylan had been the only one from his team to return—alive.

"Dylan?" his mother called from the other side of the thin door. Growing up, he shared this room with Ramey while Logan and Nick shared the other bedroom. They didn't have much growing up, but they had each other, and that, for the most part, had always been enough.

"Come in, Mom," he said.

She peeked her head inside. "Do you need anything?"

"I'm good, thanks." When his brother Ramey had taken off for West Point, the trailer had become eerily quiet with just him and his mom. Sometimes he could hear his mother crying over the loss of her beloved husband. He tried to be strong for his mother. He did what he could around the house and tried to stay out of trouble.

He also did his best to make sure he didn't worry his mother, but it had been that year that the nightmares had begun. They weren't anything like what he experienced in the last few weeks, but they weren't pleasant either. Often, he barely remembered the dream, just woke with a sudden start and an utterly helpless feeling.

The Army gave him the sense of purpose he craved and soon, those middle of the night moments faded into the abyss, except for the rare occasion he had too much time with his own thoughts.

"Logan dropped off a car for you to use, but are you sure you can drive?" His mother leaned against the doorframe, her arms folded across her chest. She'd been a force to be reckoned with his entire childhood, and without her, he wouldn't have had the courage to continue.

"Other than going to physical therapy, I don't plan

on doing much but stare at the water and maybe toss over a fishing line."

"How long do you really plan on staying?"

"I don't honestly know. Can we take it week by week?" He never wanted to hurt his mother's feelings, but he couldn't lie to her either.

"You know you can come home anytime and stay as long as you like, but I'm worried about you. They told me very little about what happened and only the bare-bones of your injuries."

He opened his mouth, but she held up her hand.

"I know you can't talk about the mission or what happened to you. I accept that, and I'm not sure I want to know. But your body took a beating, and I've done some research on brain injuries—"

"Mom," he interrupted, knowing that was some-thing she despised. "I'm getting better every day. I just need time and space to heal."

She nodded. "Promise me you'll come to me if things get worse or something doesn't feel right."

"I promise." And he meant it. He didn't have a death wish, like some thought. All he wanted was to get back in the field, and in order for the Army to let that happen, he had to get back to his normal self.

"Good night, Dylan."

"Night, Mom." He pulled the covers to his chin, rolling to his side, staring out the window at Kinsley's trailer. Talk about one hell of a sexy woman. Her eyes were the color of the ocean, and her dark hair flowed over her sun-kissed skin like a fine mink coat. The light from her family room filtered through the night, reaching like a long finger toward him. He cranked open the window, and he could hear a faint whisper coming from her television.

Now who was invading one's personal space?

He closed his eyes, allowing his mind to form a vision of her walking down the beach in a white sundress that danced in the breeze like lilies, while his ears focused on the mumbles from whatever show she had on. The idea bounced around in his mind that if he could concentrate on these two things as he drifted off to sleep, they would keep the dreams at bay.

Focusing on something so pleasant when he'd been a teenager always did the trick, so he hoped it would be true while he lay in his childhood room.

He allowed himself to enter the vision in his mind, walking next to Kinsley, taking her soft hand in his as they strolled across the beach without a care in the world. She didn't represent the need for a romantic relationship in his life, but simply trying to focus on light and fun, and maybe a little sexual distraction since he could see himself in bed with his mother's beautiful neighbor.

Anything to keep the dreams at bay.

In his mind, he'd stopped walking and tugged Kinsley to his chest, circling his arms around her waist, staring into her blue orbs, licking his lips in anticipation of taking her mouth.

Certain body parts stirred.

Back to walking and no kissing. He wanted to sleep

without having a nightmare, nothing more, nothing less. Besides, self-satisfaction wasn't high on his list of things to do. But if he dreamt it, well then, that would be okay.

So, for now, he'd continue to take a stroll with Kinsley, with his hand firmly planted on the small of her back, until he drifted off into a peaceful sleep.

Key word: peaceful.

He let his body relax as his mind focused on Kinsley. He should feel guilty for using her like this, but she'd never know.

He took in as deep a breath as he could without the sharp pain of broken ribs shocking his system, letting it out slowly through his mouth. He repeated this action five times as he let his body slowly relax. Sleep only moments away...

he sky darkened, and Kinsley faded off into the ocean, smiling and waving as if they might see each other again. "I'll be over here if you need me," she said before her silhouette disappeared over the waves crashing into the shore.

A vortex hurled his body into the dense jungle. The screams from his men being tortured burned in his ears. The sounds were like nothing he'd ever heard before. His men didn't even sound human anymore.

He glanced around the cage his captors held him in. His own body riddled with bruises, broken bones, and burning flesh. The tapping of metal against metal caught his attention as he whipped his body around.

Dad?

His father stood before him. He wore his favorite fishing T-shirt he'd gotten from the local surf shop, a pair of jean shorts, and his standard flip-flops. The only difference was he didn't smile like he normally did when Dylan spent time with him.

"Why are you here?" Dylan asked, blinking. "You don't belong here."

"Don't I?" his father said.

Dylan raised his hand and lunged forward. A sharp blade ripped through his father's body.

His father howled, screaming in pain right along with his men. The screeching tore through Dylan's brain. He tried to open his mouth to say something, but only gibberish came out.

The blade dropped to the ground, and Dylan stared at his shaking hand while his father fell to his knees, clutching his gut as blood oozed from his body like a waterfall.

From somewhere behind Dylan, the sound of electricity hitting water made his body shudder. He braced for the burn, but instead, it was his hands that applied the electric cables to his father's body.

*D*ylan screamed as he bolted to an upright position. His dreams had morphed into him torturing his men, but this was the first time his father entered the dream.

A light flicked on outside.

Great, he'd woken his neighbor.

Which meant…

"Dylan!" His mother pushed open the door and before he could wipe the sweat that had beaded across his forehead, she was sitting on the bed next to him, her warm hand over his shoulder. "Are you hurt?"

"No," he whispered, clearing his throat, trying to rid the visions of stabbing his father to death from his hazy mind. "I just had a bad dream."

"Some bad dream. I remember after your father died, you had them, but you didn't cry out like that. I thought maybe you were dying."

His pulse continued to race. If his mother had only known what he'd dreamt about, she would have chosen different words.

"The dreams, according to the doctor, are normal. I'm just reliving some of what happened to me. This too shall pass." He balled his fists in hopes it would calm his trembling body as he kissed his mother's cheek. "Go back to sleep. I'll be fine."

His mother let out a long breath. "There was nothing normal about that scream. You really should be talking to someone about this."

"I did when I was in the hospital."

"Well, you should continue. Whatever happened over there changed you." She stood, cupping his face. "You have a darkness lurking behind your eyes. It's not that same restlessness you and your brothers have had in the past. This is new and it's different, and I'm asking you to talk to someone if for no other reason than to humor your mother."

"Mom, I'm—"

"No buts, and I know just the person."

Dylan glanced at the clock. At four in the morning, he didn't want to have this discussion.

"My neighbor, Kinsley, is a doctor, and she specializes in things like this."

"I'll think about it," he said as he glanced out the window.

Kinsley's silhouette moved across the window. It might not hurt to talk to her. It wasn't like he'd see her after he went back to Delta Force and his mom moved to Orlando.

3

*K*insley slowed her pace as she walked past Catherine's trailer after her morning jog on the beach. If she couldn't afford to live on the ocean, living across the street was the next best thing.

She rounded the bend that faced the Intracoastal Waterway, stopping in front of her trailer to get the newspaper. When she flipped it open, she stared into the rich, tortured eyes of Dylan Sarich. She settled down on her front porch overlooking the water, kicked her feet up, and started reading.

A Hero Returns Home.

Major Dylan James Sarich of the United States Army and part of the special forces group, Delta Force, was injured last month in an operation to rescue three Marines that caused the loss of nine souls. Details of the mission are classified. However, in a ceremony on the Fourth of July, in Jupiter, Florida, Major Sarich will be awarded two medals:

the Medal of Honor, for his heroism in combat, and the Purple Heart, for the life-threatening wounds he suffered during combat.

Sarich was born and raised in Jupiter, Florida, where his father, Michael Edward Sarich, had been the local sheriff for twenty years until he died in the line of duty. Dylan's three brothers have all served in the military, and it is with great honor and respect, we welcome this hero, and his family, home.

Kinsley wiped the tears rolling down her cheeks. The shattering scream that had come from the Sarich trailer still sent goosebumps across her skin.

She'd only known Catherine for two months, but since the day Kinsley moved in, Catherine had done nothing but talk about her boys, her grandchildren, and her late husband. They were good people, and it broke Kinsley's heart to see such pain etched into Dylan's eyes.

"Kinsley," a familiar female voice said.

"Hi, Mrs… I mean Catherine." Kinsley respected that Catherine preferred to be referenced by her first name. "How are you this morning?"

"Happy and sad at the same time." Catherine stood at the base of the front porch, wearing a pair of leggings and a fitted shirt, showing off a trim body for a woman who had to be in her mid-fifties but didn't look a day over forty. "My other three boys and their families left early this morning to go back to Orlando."

"Must have been nice to have everyone in the same place, even if for one evening."

Catherine glanced over her shoulder and let out a long sigh. "I have a huge favor to ask."

"Sure." In the two months that Kinsley had lived in the neighborhood, she and Catherine shared happy hour cocktails once a week on Friday evenings. At first, Kinsley thought it made her look pathetic, but they were both exhausted from a long week of work, and it was a nice way to wind down, ignoring the fact that neither one of them had a man in their lives.

They didn't need one.

"I don't want to upset Dylan or embarrass him, but three times last night, he screamed in his sleep. I don't mean like a normal nightmare scream. These were something like I have never heard before."

Kinsley opted not to share with her neighbor that she'd heard at least one of those screams. "Have you asked him about them?"

Catherine nodded. "But he brushes them off as normal. He did have nightmares after his father died, but all the boys did. I spoke to his brother Nick, who lost his first wife and unborn child in a boating accident, and asked him what he thought since he suffered from nightmares for a while, but nothing like what I described. He thinks I should give Dylan some space, but, Kinsley, it was worse than listening to a baby with colic for hours on end and not being able to soothe them."

Kinsley couldn't relate to the baby thing, nor could she even understand a mother's pain as it related to their child, since her mother hadn't a clue how to parent. But Kinsley understood trauma and how it affected loved ones, and she could hear the torment in Catherine's trembling voice.

"What do you want me to do?"

"I asked him if he'd consider talking to you, so I was wondering if you might stop by and offer?"

Kinsley bit down on her tongue. She didn't like to push herself, or her profession, on friends. Being a psychiatrist, people constantly asked her opinion, and she usually gave a generic comment, but always refrained from getting too involved.

"Do you know if he's talked to anyone? A doctor that specializes in these things?" This was Kinsley's specialty, but she didn't want to step on anyone else's toes.

"He says he did in Germany, but I have his doctor schedule for the next few weeks here, and he's only seeing a physical therapist and has a follow-up with a neurologist. That's it."

"I'm sure the Army has done a full evaluation and will do one before he is allowed back into active duty." Kinsley had two retired vets as patients, plus her father spent years in the service, so she understood a little bit on how the military worked. "And it hasn't been that long since the mission. His mind is also going to need time to heal."

"He's not the same man," Catherine said with pleading eyes. "I know my boys, and they all have had their own demons to battle since their father died, but Dylan—his are darker and deeper."

Kinsley waved Catherine to join her on the porch. "What do you mean?"

"They were all very close to their father. They were the four musketeers and their dad their fearless leader. When Michael died, I did the best I could, but they all had this restlessness about them. Well, all of them but Nick, until his first wife died."

"That must have been horrible for everyone."

Catherine sat on the rocking chair, folding her hands in her lap. "Nick changed, and he quit his job as a cop and joined the military. It was good for him. Gave him purpose and brought him closer to Logan again. Those two have a special bond, like Ramey and Dylan. However, it also fed this restlessness all the boys had."

"Had?"

"Cliché, but the love of a good woman changed that with my first three."

"Not cliché, but I'm sure there is more to that than meets the eye in the sense they overcame whatever held them back from making those kind of human connections. It isn't uncommon for children, even adult children, to have problems with that when a parent dies." Or runs off with their fifth husband without a word, leaving a sixteen-year-old to fend for herself.

"I'm afraid that whatever happened on this last mission has pushed him over an edge."

"You think he could hurt himself?"

"No. No." Catherine shook her head. "But Dylan,

even more so than his daredevil brother Ramey, has always valued other lives over his own."

"How do you mean, exactly?" Kinsley should end this conversation and recommend a colleague, but after meeting the attractive man, hearing him scream, and listening to Catherine's take, Kinsley was like a doe in headlights. "As in willing to lay down his life to save another?"

"Yes. All of my boys are like that, something they got from being the sons of a police officer. But Dylan is the kind of man that wouldn't think twice about stepping in front of a speeding train to save someone even if he knew it would kill him."

"I find that is true of a lot of men and women in the military. It's in part why we honor them with medals and give them uniforms. You can't put a price on a life, yet we pay them to do so."

"But I think Dylan expects his death to happen that way, as if he's waiting for it. He was only fourteen when his father died. I was at work when one of the deputies came to the door, and Dylan was the only one home. Logan was off at college, Nick at the Police Academy, and Ramey was off with some girl, being Ramey. Dylan went to the hospital where his father died only five minutes after he'd gotten there. I found him sprawled out on the bed next to his father, and he wouldn't get up. Ramey had to pull him off the bed with force."

For the second time in less than an hour, Kinsley

found herself wiping away tears. "Did he talk to anyone after that?"

Catherine nodded. "He saw the school psychologist and other than a few problems, which were more normal teenage antics, Dylan made his way through high school and on to West Point, only I always sensed an emptiness inside him, bigger than his brothers. I think they all tried to fill their father's void with adrenaline."

"You know, you'd be very good at my job," Kinsley said, trying to lighten the mood.

"Only, I don't know how to help him, and whatever is tormenting him throughout the night scares me." Catherine leaned forward, resting her elbows on her knees. "I know it's a lot to ask, but I was hoping you'd offer him an ear."

"I'm happy to talk to him, whether it be in my office or casually, but I won't pry, and I will not report back to you."

Catherine blinked, nodding. "I'm not normally one of those meddling mothers." She pulled her hair over her shoulder, twisting it. "I only want to help my boy get through this troubling time."

"I'll let him know I'm available if he wants." Before Kinsley could stand, Dylan hobbled down the front steps of his mother's trailer.

"There you are," he said, gripping the railing with one hand and a cane with the other. He sported a pair of jeans and a white T-shirt. Red marks that looked like burns dotted his exposed skin.

"Kinsley, I'd like you to meet my youngest son, Dylan," Catherine said.

"We met yesterday, actually." Kinsley stood, offering her chair.

"Thanks." He limped across her squeaky wooden porch, scrunching his face as he sat down. "Normally, my mother would be grabbing me by the ear right now for taking a lady's seat."

"You didn't take, I offered." She leaned against the railing, trying not to stare, and it wasn't the scar on the side of his face, the burns on his arms, or the boot on his foot that caught her attention.

His smile showed a kind and warm man, but behind his shimmering, pastel-blue eyes lurked a sadness that made her shiver.

"Why don't I get us all some coffee, and I have banana bread in the oven." Catherine leapt to her feet and practically raced toward her home.

"You don't have to do that," Kinsley protested. Now was not the time to gently prod into this man's private life.

"So, I take it my screams in the middle of the night woke you up, and my mother has been over here asking you to talk to me about it."

"Yes on both accounts." No reason for her to lie. Besides, she'd already offered.

"So, what do you charge?"

"I'm not on the list for military insurance."

He let out a short laugh. "Do I need to ask the question again?"

"No," she said, tucking a strand of hair behind her ear. "Non-insurance patients, my fees are one fifty an hour."

"Do you see patients on weekends?"

"I have some Saturday appointments."

"For as long as I'm here, my mother isn't going to let this go, and she means the world to me, so I'll schedule a few appointments, but I don't want them to be in your office."

"That's unconventional and frankly, you're wasting your money, and my time, if you aren't going to take this seriously."

"I'll give it a fair shot, if you agree to see me a couple times a week," he arched a brow, "outside the office. Say, on the beach, or at dinner, or just sitting on that dock over there."

She glanced over her shoulder in the direction he pointed and swallowed. "This sounds more like you're hiring me to be an escort."

He laughed, then coughed.

When she turned back around, he clutched his side. "I'm just not comfortable talking about personal things in an office."

"It would be unethical of me to see you as a patient in any place other than my office."

"All right then," he said. "What if I just confided in you as your neighbor's son, not as a patient?"

"I can't take your money, and I'm not your therapist, but I'm happy to listen." She should say no, but she couldn't deny the emptiness that he tried to hide, and he did it pretty well. But that noise that echoed in the night made her skin crawl. Whatever haunted his dreams was so horrific that she feared if he didn't deal with it, he'd be forever changed and not in a good way.

"Thanks," he said, leaning back. "Can we start today? Say four and we can sit down on the dock, maybe have a glass of wine."

"Four works for me." She smiled. Her heart raced. He had a charm about him that would be irresistible if she wasn't careful.

"Here comes my mother," he said.

Kinsley turned her attention to Catherine, who carried a tray of coffee and loaf of fresh bread. Kinsley reached out, praying her hands didn't shake as she took the tray. "This smells delicious."

"My mom makes the best," Dylan said, slicing the bread, and taking a large piece, popping half of it in his mouth. "But I should be going. I have a busy day."

"Doing what?" Catherine asked.

Kinsley took a slice and bit into the warm bread. A mini orgasm went off in her mouth.

"I've got a date," he said.

"With who?" Catherine held her coffee mug halfway to her lips.

"Kinsley."

Kinsley coughed and gagged as half the treat lodged in her throat. "It's not a date."

---

4

*D*ylan grimaced as he carried a second lawn chair to the dock, his strength drained from merely walking across the street.

"What are you doing?" his mother called, racing across the street with a bag in one hand and a bottle of wine in the other. "I told you I'd bring everything over and don't you go bringing it back after your date. I'll take care of it."

"It's not a date, and yes, Mother, I'll leave the chairs for you to bring back." Thankfully, it was book club night for his mom. Teasing her about him going on a date had been a stupid idea. Asking Kinsley to meet him for a drink even dumber. He should cancel.

"What is it then?"

"I'm doing as you asked, and I'm going to talk to her about the dreams."

"I'm so glad. I hear she's a very good psychiatrist."

His mother helped him set up a tray of cheese,

grapes, crackers, and a nice bottle of red wine, all his mother's idea.

"And it's a beautiful night to watch the sunset," his mother said.

"It's four in the afternoon." He stretched out his leg with the boot as he twisted the corkscrew, his ribs throbbing, and his raw skin burning. It felt good to have the gauze bandages off, but his arms, chest, and back looked like someone had tried to play connect the dots with a cattle prod.

"There is a second bottle on the wine rack."

"Is this the wine we had at Mia's?" The cork slid out with a gentle pop, and he lifted it to his nose, inhaling the rich, full-bodied scent of butterscotch mixed with a hint of vanilla.

"They gave me a case for my birthday."

He laughed, shaking his head. "I'm still a beer kind of guy, but they did teach me to appreciate this stuff."

His mother ran her fingers through his hair, looking him over as only a mother could do. She'd been the family's rock, and Dylan often wished he could be a better son, but every time he came home, a few days would pass, and he couldn't wait to get back in the action. It wasn't his mother, or his family.

It was him.

He couldn't sit still or be in one place for any length of time.

"I worry about you, Dylan."

"I'm fine, Mom." He took her hand and kissed her palm.

"If I didn't think you needed to deal with…" His mother let out a long breath, and her eyes filled with tears. "You really scared me last night."

"I don't mean to frighten you, but it's not uncommon to have bad dreams after going through what I did."

"My mind goes wild on what could have happened when I look at your scars." She bent over and kissed his forehead like she used to do when he was little. "I know you can't talk to me about it, and your brothers couldn't stay since they are taking time off for the Fourth of July celebration, but whatever is going on in here," she tapped his temple, "is eating you alive, and it's breaking my heart."

It would destroy his mother if he told her that the dreams included his father. Actually, they were centered around him. "I'm not going to let it fester. I just need time."

She nodded.

The sound of a door closing caught his attention.

Kinsley glided down the front porch steps wearing a pair of red shorts that stopped a few inches above her knees, showing off a set of tanned, firm legs. Her white blouse hung off both of her shoulders and that damn raven hair bounced like the opening of the hit TV show *Baywatch* where the lifeguards ran in slow motion, captivating the audience.

"Close your mouth and stop gawking," his mother said, tugging at his ear.

"Ma, stop it." He rubbed the side of his head.

"Behave like the gentleman I raised, and I wouldn't have to do that."

"Yes, ma'am." What grown man was terrified of his mother?

The four Sarich brothers, that's who.

"You know, if I didn't feel you needed a trained professional, I'd be trying to fix you and—"

"Mom, really? We're going to go there this second?"

"Go where?" Kinsley asked with a bright smile.

His breath hitched.

He blamed it on the broken rib.

"You make sure this one behaves," his mother said, blowing a kiss as she jogged across the street, waving with a wicked smile.

Dylan let out a long breath.

"Your mother is something special." Kinsley sat in the folding chair, holding out one of the glasses.

"Yeah, she is." He filled their glasses. "Here's to my mom."

The plastic goblets clinked under the bright sun as it danced on the waterway. Growing up poor in Jupiter was an oxymoron, considering Jupiter Island has the highest concentration of wealth in the United States. His mom worked as a cleaning lady, and now owned her own cleaning company and could afford to move, but until recently, she hadn't ever thought about it.

Hopefully, she'd retire.

She worked entirely too damn hard, and it was time for her to kick back and enjoy her life.

"God, I love it here," Kinsley said, resting her head

back on the chair. Her neck stretched, and her skin begged to be kissed.

He tugged at his ear.

"Are you from the area?" He wanted to ask her age, thinking she might be close to his, but that would be rude, and this wasn't a date. This was a *listening* session. Specifically, he was supposed to be talking about his dreams, not finding out what made this chick tick.

"I've lived in West Palm and Orlando, but always loved coming here, so when I decided to open my own practice, I landed here. Being able to walk to the beach, or Ground Hog's, you can't beat that."

"No, you can't." Dylan swirled his wine, watching the dark-red liquid hug the sides. "I know your dad is still in Orlando, but what about the rest of your family?"

A sarcastic laugh filled the afternoon air. "My mother's current husband has a winter house in Boca, but they live in Jersey in the summer."

"Current?" He rolled his head. The bright rays of the sun caught her sapphire eyes. He'd never seen eyes quite that shade of blue before and with her dark hair, and slightly bronzed complexion, she had to be the most beautiful woman he'd ever laid eyes on.

"Yeah, this makes husband number six. Too bad it will end soon. I actually kind of like this guy, and he's her age instead of being my age, or older than dirt."

Dylan covered his mouth, trying not to laugh. Not just because he didn't want to insult her, but it really hurt.

"Here's something that will make you laugh. I want to fix your mother up with my dad."

"Which one?" He winced.

But she took the comment in stride, smiling, shaking her head. "The one whose sperm created me."

He grabbed his side, holding it tightly, trying to keep his damned rib from snapping in half again while laughter spewed out of his mouth like a wide-open fire hydrant. "Are you close to your dad?"

"Very." She reached for a grape and popped it into her mouth, licking her plump, pink lips. "He's the best."

"My brothers seem to like him."

She nodded. "We didn't make the connection until we heard of your accident."

"It wasn't an accident," he ground out, squeezing his fist. "It was a well-thought-out ambush, and someone had been tipped off that we were coming." He took a large gulp of wine, letting it burn his throat, kicking up his heartburn. The smell of death seeped into his nostrils like the stench of a landfill in the hot summer sun.

"Is that what haunts you in your sleep? The ambush?"

"It's with me day and night, but only a small part of the nightmare," he said behind a clenched jaw. The desire to retreat into silence and change the subject pelted his gut like stones kicking up from a gravel road under monster tires. "Do you interpret recurring dreams?"

"I've studied dreams and dream analysis, but I

usually try not to focus too much on the dream or what's in it, other than feelings, at least at first."

"Why is that?" His nightmare was so vivid, that every time he snapped awake, he had to blink the visions away, only they didn't leave.

"Let's say your dream includes a machine gun. Generally speaking, people will see that as an act of aggression, so they would say, you're angry at someone or yourself. If you're shooting the gun, it could represent the need to kill destructive behaviors, not that you want to kill anyone."

"Sounds like a lot of psycho-babble." There were guns in his dreams, but he doubted that's what they meant.

"Exactly and often by focusing on the actions, or objects, or even people in a dream, we misread what the mind is trying to do." She crossed her ankles as she took a sip of her wine. "Can I assume you spoke to a therapist before coming to Jupiter?"

"I did as required when coming off any mission where actual combat is involved. They ask standard questions, I give honest responses."

"But you don't elaborate," she said, keeping her gaze on the water.

"I do not," he admitted. "They did ask me about the dreams, as I had them in hospital, freaking out half the staff. But they started out as a replay of hearing my men being tortured to death."

"Any normal man would have nightmares," she said, shifting her chair and looking him square in the eye. "I know good men died, but I don't know the details. Maybe if I did, I could help more."

"It's all classified." He raised his glass before downing the last few drops and pouring another hefty serving. "I can't discuss the details with you; I've said too much as it is."

"All right. I'll work with what I do know, but before I ask my set of probing questions, did they give you medication for PTSD?"

"I'm not taking it. I know I have all the classic signs, but the neurologist says I shouldn't take it until we know more about other symptoms."

"What symptoms?"

"I've had balance issues, memory problems, and I didn't do well on an exam that I'm an expert in, but that was two weeks ago and I'm much better."

"When is your follow-up appointment?"

"Next week," he said.

"Brain trauma could very well be affecting your dreams," she said. "You mentioned recurring. For how long?"

"When I was younger, I had some dreams after my father died. It was always about not being able to save him, or anyone else in the dream. They mostly went away, though occasionally came back when I'd return home from a mission. But now I dream about my men being tortured. It was always the same until about a week ago."

"Did the dream completely change, or just new elements?" She spoke in an even tone. The timbre of her voice floated over his ears like drizzling honey coating a slice of warm bread, making him feel at ease.

"My father was added."

"How so?"

"I keep killing my father over and over again. With every scream I hear from my men, I kill my dad in my dream." He closed his eyes tight. Did he really just admit to that? It had to be the most fucked-up dream any man could ever have.

"That's an interesting twist, considering your father has been dead for over ten years."

"Twist?" He jerked his head, arching his back, and groaned as his muscles revolted against the quick moment. "That's a weird reaction."

"Sorry. I didn't mean to offend you. It's just that killing someone in your dream doesn't necessarily mean you want to kill them, or want them dead, but a manifestation of an event, in this case, the mission, and how it relates to the death of your father."

He opened his mouth three or four times, but nothing came out. Her analysis made way too much sense and was so simple, but that didn't change the way it made him feel as if he'd been the one to pull the trigger the day his father died.

Or the man who handed his men's captors weapons of horror.

"They don't relate at all," he said.

"Sure, they do. People died. That's connection enough." She leaned over, plucking a few crackers and cheese chunks off the plate. "Will you try something for me?"

"What's that?" he asked, terrified she wanted to do something crazy like hypnotize him.

"I want you to keep a dream journal. As soon as you're awake, write down what you can remember from the dream and how each element made you feel. Make sure you date the entries and if you wake multiple times in a night, put down the time as well."

"What if I feel numb inside?"

"Write it down."

"You don't think that would be weird, or bad?" he asked. Not that he felt numb, but he did feel like a freak. Didn't matter that many good soldiers went through something similar.

He wasn't just any soldier, and he should be able to push past this.

"Dreams are our subconscious, not our waking minds."

"How is keeping a journal going to help?" The shrink he'd spoken to at the hospital also mentioned keeping track of the dreams, but they were so vivid, he couldn't bring himself to write them down.

"If you focus on your emotions in the dream, sometimes it shows us what is really upsetting to us in the real world. But I also want you to write down your actions."

"These dreams are not for the faint of heart," he said.

"I've heard it all and have had my share of screwed-up dreams. I think it's important for you to step outside of the nightmare and look at it from a different point of view, and the best way is to write it down. Also, if the dream is changing, focusing on the new details could be telling."

"I suppose I can give it a try."

"I want you to understand that some of this may have to do with your head injury, so keep that in mind as we talk about your entries. One other thing I want you to do is to keep track of all your symptoms. Date. Location. Time. Even things like what you had to eat or drink."

"Why?"

"Will you do it?"

"I will if you tell me about a fucked-up dream you've had."

She held her empty glass of wine out to him. "I'm going to need another glass of wine after telling you this, but maybe it will help you understand that it's not always the actions in the dream." She pushed a lock of hair back behind her shoulder.

He set the bottle on the ground, making himself a few cheese crackers. "So, hit me with your dream."

"This is probably going to be the weirdest thing you've ever heard."

He enjoyed how her cheeks flushed red and her sapphire eyes danced in the sun. He could sit here with her forever and not think twice about what he shared.

And that thought scared the hell out of him.

"I don't know about that. My brothers and I have some pretty weird real stories."

"All right, I'll tell you this if you tell me the most embarrassing thing you've ever done."

"Deal." What the fuck? Why did he just agree to that?

"I sometimes dream I'm a guy and I'm having sex, with a woman," she said so fast he had to stick his finger in his ear.

"Say what?"

"It's not that uncommon of a dream."

"I've never heard of anyone else having that dream," he said, patting his chest in beat with his erratically pounding heart. He wanted to reach out and hold her hand.

Just hold it.

That was weird.

He wasn't a ladies' man. He wasn't a womanizer. He just didn't have time for relationships, so, he had a few women he knew that were friends with benefits. Though, most of them had since moved on to relationships, turning him down when he called.

He respected that.

"What does it mean?" he asked, hoping it didn't mean she was secretly a lesbian. Not that he wouldn't respect that either, but he wanted... nope, not going there.

"It could mean a lot of things, but it generally has to do with needing to incorporate some qualities often associated with the opposite sex."

"What does it mean for you, exactly?" He took a large sip of courage.

"I can be a bit of a pushover, so I believe it has to do with being more assertive and my own advocate."

"How can you be sure?"

"Because I have the dream whenever my mother breaks up with her latest love." She took a slow, but long sip. "Your turn."

"Well, since we're talking sex. A girlfriend I had in high school, well, we sent…you know…naked selfies to each other and when we broke up, she hacked my Facebook account and posted the pictures I sent her."

"You're kidding?"

Dylan enjoyed how Kinsley's eyes went wide with amusement and the corners of her mouth tipped upward in a sweet smile.

"Nope. And if that wasn't embarrassing enough, my mother saw them and believed I actually posted them."

"Oh, dear Lord," she said, covering her mouth. "I'd be mortified."

"I was for about five minutes." He winked. "Your turn."

"Nuh-uh. I told you something embarrassing already." She shook her head, sending her dark locks bouncing over her shoulders. He'd found most women to be attractive, but there was something so special about Kinsley.

He didn't know what it was, and it wasn't tied up in her looks.

"Fair enough," he said, eyeing a pelican flying low

over the waterway, while trying to tame his thoughts of the sexy lady breathing the same air. "You hungry?"

"I need to eat dinner at some point," she said.

"Want to walk across the street to Windsor's?"

"Can you handle walking?" she asked with an arched brow.

"If you help hold me up."

5

$\mathcal{D}$ ylan clutched his side, wondering if he rebroke his rib. He gasped to fill his lungs with oxygen. Perspiration coated his skin. A light flicked on in Kinsley's trailer, and he could hear his mother milling about. He'd told her that unless he called for her, he would appreciate being left alone with his thoughts.

He flicked on the light and snagged the journal Kinsley had given him and stared at the blank page. If he did as she asked, he'd have to start with his thoughts before he fell asleep. Screw it, he started writing.

$\mathcal{I}$ 'm walking on the beach with Kinsley. Just enjoying the sunset. I want to feel peaceful before I drift off, hoping it will stop the nightmare.

It never does, and tonight was no exception.

I think I'm asleep when I watch Kinsley walk out into the

ocean, waving, her feet gliding across the waves. She tells me she's here if I need her. This is the second time she's been in this part of the dream. I don't know if that is significant, but I worry that I'll start pulling her into the nightmare.

This time, the sky goes dark, and I see my father walking toward me. We're not in captivity, but on the beach. However, I can still hear my men screaming. I swear, I can smell their burning flesh. I know they are dying. I can hear them calling for their wives, children, mothers.

I raise my hand and stab my father over and over again.

What is weird, this time, is that my brothers are standing off in background, watching.

I feel anger toward my brothers. They aren't doing anything to stop me from hurting our dad. I feel sadness when I look at my dad, but he has this weird smile on his face.

Right before I wake up, I realize I no longer hear the heartbeat of one of my men.

*H*e reread the words, but he didn't edit, or add, like Kinsley had asked him. If he was going to get back to Delta Force, he had to trust someone with this shit, and Kinsley was it. He couldn't tell all this to a shrink in the Army. That would be career suicide.

His phone vibrated.

. . .

*K*insley: Are you writing in your journal?

Dylan: I take it I woke you up again.

Kinsley: That's what I get for sleeping with the window open. Answer my question.

Dylan: I just finished.

Kinsley: Try to go back to sleep but use a different feel good trigger.

Dylan: It never works.

Kinsley: But it helps you fall asleep, and no matter how bad the dreams are, your mind and body are never going to heal unless you get some shut-eye.

Dylan: Night, Kinsley.

*H*e laughed, setting the phone on the table and clicked off the light. He glanced out the window and gasped, staring at Kinsley. She stood in front of her own window and waved before shutting off her light, making the moon in the sky the only light.

For the next two hours, he tossed and turned. He knew he fell asleep a couple of times, but something always jerked him awake. It wasn't the dream, but something dark tickled the back of his mind.

No. If he was being honest, it was an overwhelming sense of fear that kept him from sleeping. He made note of it in his journal before heading into the shower and then to the kitchen.

His mother sat at the table with the newspaper and a mug. "You're up awfully early."

He pulled down the ointment from the cabinet and started rubbing it over his burns. He did his best to cover the discomfort, but by the scrunched-up look on his mother's face, he didn't mask his pain very well.

"Let me do that," his mother said softly.

He sat at the table while his mother put the creamy lotion on the burns and cuts his captors had carved into his body. A constant reminder of how he'd failed his men.

"I can drive you to physical therapy this morning, if you'd like."

"I can manage. I also want to go to the bookstore. Kinsley recommended a couple of books for me to read."

His mother stepped in front of him, standing between the kitchen and the family room. "I'm glad you feel comfortable talking with her."

"She has a way of making me think, though I haven't decided if that is good or bad." He snagged his T-shirt, pulling it carefully over his head. His ankle throbbed from overuse, even in the boot. But he had to push hard, both with his body.

And his mind.

"When you were a baby, your father used to call you the stinker thinker because you always sported this serious look."

"Guess I should be glad that Baby Dyl took and not that nickname."

"Baby Dyl is how we named you Dylan." His mother let out a quiet laugh. "Logan may look the most like your father, but you," she turned, clutching the picture to her chest, "are the most like him."

"Mom. We all have different traits from both you and Dad." He feared if he talked too much about his dad, then the dreams would just intensify, and he couldn't take much more of the torment of killing his father in a nightmare.

She held out her hand. "Yes. I can see a piece of Dad in all you boys. Even in the grandkids, I can see his legacy. But he died when you were so young, and sometimes I wonder if you never really got the chance to really feel how proud he was of you. How proud he'd be of the man you've become."

"I know he was and would be," Dylan said, hobbling toward his mother. It was still difficult without his cane, but he managed well enough.

"His death hit all of us hard. But I always worried the most about you."

"Mom, really. I had a great childhood and the best mom ever."

She smiled, setting the picture down. "I know I did the best I could, but you hold the pains of the world in your heart. Your father often did the same thing. I remember when he was called to his first domestic violence crime. He was so distraught over the poor woman who refused his help."

"She was murdered less than a year later by her husband." Dylan remembered the story well. His father used to tell all his boys that a man who hits a woman is no man at all. "Dad had enormous empathy for everyone. He was the kind of man who would give his last dollar to a perfect stranger."

"So are you."

"So are all my brothers," he said.

"But none of them had nightmares like you or your dad," she said, tilting her head with an arched brow. "He didn't like to talk about it, but he struggled the first few years in the police department. He almost quit, had it not been for a therapist who helped him cope with all that he was feeling when he thought he let anyone down."

Dylan's lungs expanded with oxygen, but he couldn't exhale. He blinked, staring at his mother. There was no one better than his father. He and his brothers used to talk about it late at night, how lucky that they had it, even though they didn't have things, they had great parents.

"So, this is why you told Kinsley about my nightmares."

"The difference between you and your father is that he wore his emotions on his sleeve. When he felt something, we all felt it. You swallow them whole, letting them sit in your gut, never to be discussed. To most people in your path, they see a strong man who is constantly in control. They see an honorable, caring man." She stepped closer, patting his chest. "But they also see an emptiness in you and that started long before this mission."

He stared into his mother's soft-blue eyes. Anger tickled his brain. But like always, he kept that in check. It never paid to go off half-cocked. Logic trumped everything.

He wasn't void of emotions, and his only problem was that he'd been injured in such a way that it affected his thinking. Once he had a chance to heal, his mind, and his dreams, he would go back to normal.

Only, he realized, his dreams had always been horrifying, even when they didn't wake him up.

"You know I'm right," his mother said.

"I'm working on it." He swallowed, hard. The swirling of utter loneliness he'd felt when he watched his father take his last breath, squeezed his aching heart. Flashes of every man he'd ever served with that had perished pelleted his mind like rapid fire. Breathing in through his nose, and letting it out slowly, he did exactly what his mother accused him of.

He ate every negative feeling he had, leaving him only with guilt.

K insley sat on the stairs of her porch, trying not to turn her head to every car that turned the corner, hoping it would be the Jeep that Dylan had borrowed. Between patients, all she could think about was Dylan and his dreams. He'd yet to share the specifics of his latest dreams, but in their few text messages, he mentioned feeling as though he were off-kilter. He hadn't elaborated, but he said he'd come over when he got back from the store.

What the hell was he doing at the store? He could barely walk without assistance.

She sipped her wine, wondering why she'd opened another bottle.

Nerves.

But why did Dylan make her so skittish?

A black Jeep rolled to a stop under Catherine's carport. Dylan hobbled out, waving. "I hate to ask, but can you give me a hand?"

She started clapping. What a stupid fucking thing to do.

But Dylan let out a belly laugh. "Not that kind of a hand."

"What do you need?"

"Mind carrying in our dinner?" He leaned against his cane, carrying a bottle of white wine in his other hand.

"I didn't agree to dinner," she said as she pulled open the back door of the vehicle and snagged a to-go bag from the Reef Bar and Restaurant.

"But you have to eat, and my mom is helping Mrs. Vanderlin with a fundraiser, and I don't want to eat alone."

She hip-checked the door. "Does this have something to do with feeling a bit off today?"

"It might. Where shall we eat? My place or yours?"

"Mine," she said, jogging up the stairs to her porch.

She set the bags on the outside table. "I'll go get some plates and a wine glass for you."

"I see you already started on some."

"Yeah, well, I had a long day." Of worry for him, but he didn't need to know that. She collected the necessary items and took a moment to take in a calming breath. She'd be lying if she tried to tell herself she wasn't attracted to Dylan intellectually and physically. Even though he wasn't technically a patient, it would be wrong for her to pursue anything beyond friendship. Not to mention, he would be back at work, traveling the globe, putting his life at risk on a daily basis.

A lifestyle she didn't want.

When she stepped back onto the porch, he sat at the table, rubbing his temples. Quietly, she set the plates and utensils down and poured him a glass of wine. "Want to talk about it?"

"My mother said something to me today that has me confused."

Kinsley found it interesting that he used the word confused. By definition, that either meant bewilderment or not in possession of one's faculties.

She suspected he didn't mean either, and he just used the term to cover up his real ones. Though he might not exactly know what those were since he stuffed them so far deep inside.

"What was it?"

"She mentioned my father had nightmares."

"We all have them," she said, sitting down across from him, and began to serve up dinner which consisted of a couple pieces of crusted salmon, whipped potatoes, and mixed vegetables. It smelled like a little piece of heaven wrapped in a Cinnabon.

"Yeah, but she made it seem like his were related to the things he saw on the job, but he somehow managed to put it in perspective or something or other."

She leaned back in the chair. "That's not what you're confused about. You know everyone has bad dreams, especially in your line of work, and your father's. So, what is really bothering you?"

"You're pushy," he muttered before taking a sip of his wine, followed by a large piece of salmon.

"I'm just trying to help," she said, picking at her food. While she knew she was being far from pushy, she'd give him his feelings. It was the first time she'd seen them outside of him discussing the mission, his men, or his nightmares.

The night sounds filled the silence. She could be a patient woman and would wait until he was ready.

She didn't have to wait more than five minutes.

"We always knew when my father was disappointed or proud. Happy or angry. Sad or scared. There wasn't an emotion he was afraid of showing, and he always told us boys through thick and thin, family first, no matter what."

"You all have incredibly strong bonds. That's a good thing, and you all have great honor and respect for your parents and each other. It's unique."

He nodded, swirling the liquid in his glass as though he were a connoisseur of fine wines. Dylan was a bit of an oxymoron. Refined, yet rough around the edges. He came from humble beginnings, and stayed there, but what he did for a living was anything but a humble existence.

"I've always been there for my brothers, and they for me. But it usually comes in the form of adrenaline."

"I disagree." She set her fork on the plate and caught his gaze. "Your mom told me how you've tried to come home shortly after each of your nieces and nephews have been born, and they were all here for you when you returned home." She looked deep inside his blue orbs, but he gave up almost nothing. It wasn't that he was emotionless, far from it, but he kept them so tight to his chest, he didn't even know they were there, much less what they were. "I feel like you're dancing around whatever it is that your mother said that has troubled you."

He let out a sarcastic laugh. "You really don't pull any punches. Are you like this with all your clients?"

"You're not a patient, and I told you I'd always be honest, but I can't help if you keep avoiding."

"My mother told me the main difference between me and my dad is the fact that I show almost no emotion, and I kind of have to agree with her. I didn't realize it, but you asked me to write down my feelings in my dream, and God, it's pathetic. I mean, I wrote, I feel angry. What the fuck is that?"

"Let me answer that with a question." She wiped her mouth with a napkin before tossing it on the empty plate. "Do you get angry?"

"Sure."

"And what do you do?"

"I don't understand the question?"

Of course he didn't because she figured his idea of being angry was stuffing it while shooting up the sky with gunfire. "Do you yell? Slam the door? Actually, when your ex-girlfriend posted those naked pictures, were you angry and if so, what did you do?"

"Of course it ticked me off, but what could I do? Yelling doesn't solve the problem. Nor does tossing things across a room."

"So, you shrugged it off."

"Yeah."

"And when others have angered you? Do you shrug it all off as if it doesn't bother you? Or do you say something and deal with the emotion?"

"I don't hold grudges."

"Neither do I, but trust me when I say I get pissed off. If and when I'm ever ticked at you, you'll know it."

"I'll remember that and try not to anger you," he said with a teasing tone.

She found it fascinating how he waffled between a tough breakthrough with his emotions and shutting them right the fuck down. She'd seen it many times in her patients. Normally she'd wait it out, letting the client figure things out slowly, but something told her that Dylan already knew, he just wasn't willing to admit it.

"Do you have a best friend?" she asked.

"A what?"

"Someone you confide in. Tell your inner secrets. Share things that no one else knows."

"That would be my brothers."

She shook her head. "Outside of family."

He glanced to the sky, as if it had all the answers. "I don't really have time for casual or even really close relationships, so I keep my circle tight."

"As human beings, we're built to share our existence with others. You isolate yourself, which is why expressing your emotions has become nearly impossible. I'm not surprised that all your deep emotions are coming out in a dream state."

"All of this jibber-jabber is giving me a headache."

"Why don't we call it a night. We can talk again tomorrow," she said.

"I'm sorry. I don't mean to be difficult."

She reached out and placed her hand over his, rubbing her thumb over his callused skin. In the few short days she'd known him, she felt a closeness that didn't make sense. They barely knew each other, yet she could see how hard he tried to push through the barriers he'd built around himself to protect his heart from whatever it was that broke it in the first place. "Trust me, you're not difficult at all, and I enjoyed tonight."

His lips curled upward in a genuine smile. "You're something special, Kinsley."

"No need to flatter me."

"Talk again when you get home from work?"

"Sure." He stood, bending over the table, and kissed her cheek. "Thanks. You're a very kind woman."

She let out a long breath as she watched him waltz from her patio to his mother's. He stood by his front door and waved.

Well shit, she was falling for Dylan.

Hard.

6

_T_he next morning, Kinsley made her way back from her morning walk on the beach. She'd slept with her window closed, and she hadn't heard Dylan scream out in the middle of the night, but that didn't mean he hadn't had a bad dream.

She'd been surprised by how much he so easily shared with her, and more shocked by her own confessions. But it was the closeness she felt for him that made her stomach flutter like a million butterflies.

"Good morning," Dylan's voice startled her when she rounded the corner.

He sat on the steps on his front porch with a mug of coffee, in nothing but a pair of jeans tucked into his boot.

She sucked in a breath, trying not to stare.

"Want some coffee?" He nodded to a second mug on the stoop, filled with a steaming hot brew.

"I'm not one to pass on a good cup of Joe." Sitting

down next to him, she blew into the mug and stared out at the Intracoastal. A slight breeze rippled the water. She avoided relationships because she found herself becoming bored easily.

Like her mother.

Last person on earth she aspired to be like, but perhaps some things were just in one's genetic make-up, and there wasn't a damn thing they could do about it.

"Where's your mom?" she asked.

"She's already left for work."

"I've never met anyone quite like Catherine," she said, sipping the dark, almond-flavored liquid. "I have to honestly say, I have a pang of jealousy."

"About what?" He turned his head, stretching out his long legs, wincing as he twisted his upper body.

"I know my mom loves me, in her weird way, but she's a selfish woman."

"My mother's not selfish enough," he said.

"But she's got to be the most genuine, happiest person I've ever met."

"I can't argue that point." He cast a wicked smile and winked. "Thank you for listening last night."

"My pleasure," she said.

"You've helped me a lot." He shifted closer, resting his finger on her knee, drawing a small circle over her skin. "I like being around you. I feel safe."

She glanced at his hand, and then caught his gaze.

"Sorry, that was very forward of me," he said,

cupping his mug with both hands. "I find myself liking you more than I want to."

"I think I'll take that as a compliment." She lusted after him more than she'd ever admit, even to herself. Sleep hadn't come easy the last few nights, and when she did manage to fade off into oblivion, he joined her in her subconscious.

"I don't know how long I'm staying," he said.

"Your mom said two months." Why did it matter how long he was going to stay? They would never be any more than friends.

He let out a slight laugh. "I have two months of medical leave if I need it. I don't plan on needing it. And I love my mom, more than anything, but I can't stay here that long. I get too restless."

Now he sounded like her mother. Every time she left a husband, it was because she'd grown restless and bored.

Every time Kinsley had the makings of a serious relationship, she got cold feet and made like her mother, without the craziness of being married.

That's how she was different.

Right.

"But I still want to go out with you again, which makes me a selfish prick." He ran his thumb over her cheekbone before tucking her hair behind her ear. "Because I also want you to continue to help me."

She swallowed her breath, biting down on her lower lip.

"I don't do relationships." His voice boomed out

firm, and a tad harsh, though she relished in his honesty.

"I'm not looking for one," she said, curling her fingers around his wrist. "I enjoy your company, so let's just roll with it." Her heart floated in her chest like she was standing at the opening of an airplane, waiting to jump, so she could plummet to her death.

He leaned in, pressing his mouth against hers in a soft kiss that lasted only a few seconds. "Dinner tonight?"

"What about your mother?"

"She won't be back until at least eight, so I'm on my own." His hot breath tickled her skin.

"An early dinner, I have a patient at seven thirty tomorrow morning."

"Perfect," he whispered, his warm lips brushing over hers as she ran her hand up his back, stopping on one of his scars.

He jerked his head back. "I was wondering if you'd comment on them or not."

"I didn't say anything, and why would I?"

"Because they are hideous."

"I wouldn't say that, and they are still healing," she said, running her fingers across his flesh. Every scar and burn told a story.

One she found herself wanting and needing to know.

"Do you want to talk about them?" she asked, staring into his eyes, wishing she could somehow detach herself from emotion other than empathy.

"When you're tortured, you'll say anything to have the pain stop."

"Tortured? Does your mother know that?"

"I'm sure she suspects, but I can't really discuss the mission or what happened."

"Did you tell your captors things you shouldn't have?" She squeezed his shoulder before taking her mug and sipping carefully. His dreams could be dealing with so many different layers, it might take more than a few weeks to peel them back, giving him the peace of mind he searched for.

"I told them what they wanted to hear, whether it was true or not."

"Were you and your men in the same room, or separated?" She asked the kinds of questions as if he were any other patient. Only, he wasn't a patient.

And he'd just kissed her.

"They separated us, beating us at different times, telling us that one of us gave them information, and they then were given food and water."

"When you gave them information, did they give you those things?"

"No, and I knew they wouldn't." He ran a hand over his freshly shaven face. "I did what I thought was right to save my men and stop the pain, but I failed."

She reached out, resting her hand on his knee. His muscle twitched.

"You didn't fail," she said.

"But I did."

"Maybe the mission, but you didn't fail your men."

He shook his head. "I've had other failed missions and lost other good men, just not nine at once."

"You feel responsible for them?" She probed further into his mind.

"Wouldn't you?" He stared at her with darkness swirling in his blue eyes.

"I would," she admitted. She had one patient commit suicide and one die of an accidental overdose. Both times, she had to see a therapist, trying to reconcile if she could have done anything different.

Probably not, but that doesn't change the outcome.

"Did you dream last night?" she asked.

He nodded. "I wrote it all down and tried to express my feelings about it, but this one was just so weird."

"Why?"

He shrugged. "Come here, I want to show you something."

Pushing himself to a standing position, he held out his hand.

She stared at it for a long moment before resting her palm against his callused one and followed him into the family room.

Dylan handed her a picture frame that held an image of him as a boy, with his brothers and an older man, who she assumed to be his father, and Catherine.

"You look the most like your mom," she said.

"I know." He handed her another photograph. "This was taken the day before my dad died."

She held the image of a young Dylan with all of his brothers, standing on the very dock where they had drinks last night, holding a large Mahi Mahi fish in his hand. His father had his arm proudly draped over his shoulders, smiling.

"That night Logan went back to college and Nick drove off to the Police Academy. The next day, Ramey found out he'd been accepted into West Point. He'd gone off with some chick after school to celebrate, and I came home because back then, I didn't have swagger like Ramey."

She held her breath. Knowing the rest of the story didn't make it any easier.

"Last night, instead of stabbing my father, I tortured him…" he ran his hand over his chest, his fingers circling the scars… "I'm electrocuting and water-boarding my dad. What the fuck does that mean? I loved my dad, and we had a great relationship." The tightness in his voice tugged at her heart. "I feel like I'm going crazy. Like I'm losing control, and I'm always in control."

"What's going on in that nightmare isn't a reflection of your relationship with your father or how much you loved him."

"That's not even the worst of it." He turned his back, resting his hands on his hips.

"What do you mean?" She inched up behind him, resting her hand on his shoulder. "What else happened in the dream?"

"My brothers were there and waiting for me to torture them next, and my father was begging me not to hurt them, yelling 'one for all and all for one.'" He shifted his stance, glancing down at her. "This shit has to stop before I lose my fucking mind."

"How do you feel when you wake up?" The woman in her wanted to hold him and tell him everything was all right, but the psychiatrist, and the friend, knew that's not what he needed.

"How the fuck do you think I feel?" he asked, glaring.

"Physically, or emotionally?" She knew this was a dangerous game she was playing, but he had to bring his emotions to the surface and anger was always the first to roar.

"What the fuck kind of question is that?" He shrugged her hand away, crossing his arms over his chest.

"An important one, so please answer." Not only was the answer important, but how he lashed out at her could help begin the healing process.

"Both," he said with a tight jaw.

"But what do you focus on the second you wake up? Is it your racing heart? Perspiration? Jittery hands? Or is it some gut-wrenching emotion you can't even label?"

He slammed his hand down on the back of the sofa. "Jesus Christ. Will you just fucking stop the psycho-babble bullshit?"

"Dylan," she said in a firm, but soft voice. "Tell me how you felt this morning after the nightmare."

"I felt angry," he whispered. "Rage. Out of control rage. I want to hurt someone, only in my dreams I was hurting the people I love the most, and that is totally fucked up."

"No, actually, it's not," she said, giving his biceps a reassuring squeeze. "Sit down."

"I'd rather stand."

"Too bad," she said, pointing to the sofa.

Instead of sitting across from him, she eased herself on the sofa, only about twelve inches away.

Mistake. She knew it, but she no longer cared. This man was torturing himself, and his dream would never go away until he stopped beating himself up emotionally.

"One of the reasons I wanted you to keep a journal is so we... I mean you, can rifle through your subconscious until you uncover the heart of the problem."

"Why do you think I keep having these dreams? Please tell me, because I really want to know." The creases in his forehead deepened.

"I think you love your family very much. I think you'd do anything to help keep them safe."

"So, why I am doing those horrible things to my dad?"

"Listen," she said, reaching out and taking his hand in hers in a bold gesture. "There could be a million reasons why, subconsciously, like being angry at your father for dying, or feeling responsible for his death, or letting him down somehow, and that's why he's being pulled into the horror of the mission."

"And my brothers? Why are they there, but not my mom?" He closed his eyes for a long moment before blinking them open. "I'd really lose my shit if she showed up."

"It could be that you equate your men dying as part of your family and feeling responsible. It could be you're afraid you will let your brothers down."

"I'm more afraid of disappointing my mother than my brothers."

"If you continue to write down the dreams, and your emotions, something will reveal itself to you." She tried to tug her hand away, but he held it tighter.

"You really believe that?"

"I do," she said. "When I was little, I kept having this dream over and over again about drowning. I'd be at the beach, which is my happy place, and all of a sudden, a wave would come out of nowhere and take me out to sea. In the dream, I couldn't swim to the surface and I'd feel myself stop breathing, and then the ocean would go calm. That's when I'd wake up."

"And what does that dream mean?" he asked with a slight curl of his lips as if he were amused.

He was pushing his emotions down again, but they had made progress, so she'd let him sink his feelings into the abyss.

"I didn't understand until I realized that it happened every time my mother left a husband. I'd start to actually like them, and they'd leave. The dream had to do with the feeling of helplessness and loss of making connections. Bonds."

"Do you analyze all your dreams?"

She shook her head. "I do keep a journal of them,

though. Dreams can reveal a lot about our emotions. How we see ourselves and the people around us, but you can overthink all this shit, so it's important to understand that dreams are just our thoughts and often they are meshed together into things that will never make sense. I mean, we dream all night, and they can get confused as they blend into one not-so-succinct memory."

"You know, I had more than one dream last night." He leaned closer, licking his lips. "I dozed off on the sofa thinking about you."

"Really? And what were you thinking?" Totally an inapposite question, since she knew exactly where he was headed.

"This." He pulled her close, slipping his tongue between her parted lips. He tasted like coffee and cream. He felt like warm honey melting over a piece of sourdough bread still hot from the oven.

"You're changing the subject," she whispered.

"You don't seem to mind." He deepened the kiss as he leaned back on the sofa, her chest pressed against his.

He groaned, clutching his side.

She jumped off the sofa. "Yeah, not only is your body not ready for me to be lying on top of it, I'm not ready to be making out on your mother's sofa."

"We both just need a couple of days."

"I'm not sure any amount of time will make me feel comfortable with the latter."

"I'm going to make it my personal mission to make

sure more necking happens right here." He patted the sofa.

She let out a short laugh. "I've got to get to work and then run some errands. Do you need anything?"

He shook his head. "I've got physical therapy and then I'm going to binge-watch some weird shit on Netflix while I wait for you to return for our next date."

"I've lost my mind," she said.

"Be careful, because you might make me lose my heart."

7

_D_ylan had never been so grateful to have a date cancel on him, a couple of times. It wasn't that he didn't want to see Kinsley, but after making the stupid comment about having feelings for her, he needed a few days to recover from his diarrhea of the mouth.

And bleeding heart.

But only because his insides were all twisted, and he was letting her pretty face and sweet demeanor distract him from facing his demons head on.

He'd seen Kinsley a few times in passing when she'd come home from work, and he'd honestly done the best he could to avoid her over the last few days, but his dreams had gotten worse and worse.

And now his mother was in there, and he couldn't close his eyes for fear of watching himself hurt her.

He lay on the dock, staring at the night sky speckled with a million stars. He replayed every bad dream he could remember from childhood into his early years in the Army. When his father died, he used to dream that Logan had died too. He chalked that up to Logan being the oldest and the one who did what he could to kick Dylan in the ass when it came to school or not giving their mom a hard time during those turbulent adolescent years.

After Nick's first wife died, when he did have a bad dream, it was always his mother standing over his grave, and she would sob like he'd never heard before. Just thinking about the sound made him want to jump out of his skin.

He didn't need a dream to tell him that in the back of his mind, he worried about himself, or anyone in his family, dying, yet they all took on jobs that put their lives at a high risk for injury and death.

Besides, people died every day. It was a normal part of life.

"Fuck it," he mumbled, taking out his phone. He had to talk this through with someone and he trusted Kinsley, though he had no idea why. But the dreams had to be under control before he left to go back to Ft. Bragg.

 *ylan: R U up?*

e set the phone on his chest, figuring she'd already gone to bed, since it was after eleven on a work night, and his efforts were futile. He'd have to wait until morning, but his cell buzzed right away.

*K*insley: Yes. Everything okay?
Dylan: Can't sleep.
Kinsley: Dreams getting to you?
Dylan: Yes.
Kinsley: Come over.
Dylan: Ok.

*H*e stood, feeling a little less pain than the day before. With every rising of the sun, his body got stronger and stronger.

Now he just needed his mind to follow the same game plan.

She greeted him at the door with a smile and a glass of red wine. "Sorry I've been so busy, but between my mother's break up and work, I've been slammed."

"No worries," he said, taking the cobbler and following her into the trailer. Hers was a two-bedroom, and one of the smaller ones in the park, but it had one of the nicer views. "How is your mom?"

"Filled with drama, but I give her, at tops, two months before she's got another man dropping to one knee, begging for her hand in marriage. I'm just glad she decided to stay at the Jupiter Resort. Don't get me wrong, I love my mom, but she's really high-maintenance and a trailer park is beneath her."

"I got that my entire life," Dylan said, gently closing the screen door behind him. "I once took out a girl who, when she found out where I lived, wouldn't even look at me at school. What was really funny, though, was she lived in the condos next door."

"I looked at renting in there. A lot less than here."

"Exactly." He laughed. "How long is your mom staying in Jupiter?"

"I hope not long," she said. "And I won't be introducing you to her either. She would put us in a church and married yesterday."

"Don't ever let her meet my mother then, or we'll be in deep shit."

"I know, right?"

He swallowed a large gulp of wine before taking a seat on the sofa. The only light in the room glowed from the television, which had been muted. "I'm sorry to bother you."

"It's no bother. I've felt bad that I haven't been able to talk to you and had to cancel our date."

"No need to feel bad. I understand." He wasn't about to admit he'd been avoiding her because he'd found himself so attracted to her that he couldn't tell the difference between wanting her help.

And wanting her.

"So, tell me, what's on your mind?" She tucked her feet up under her adorable ass. She wore a thin T-shirt and a pair of boxer-type shorts that showed off her

lean legs. Her hair had been pulled into a messy ponytail on top of her head, and he suspected not an ounce
of makeup lined her gorgeous face.

"The dreams are getting worse and worse. I took a
nap today and woke up in a cold sweat." He glanced
around the room, avoiding her gaze. Her trailer was
scantly decorated with the bare necessities.

A couch, recliner, end and coffee tables with a small
television standing on a hutch. A few coastal paintings
on the walls, but he didn't see a single picture of family
anywhere.

Even he had pictures in his bunk at Ft. Bragg.

And in his wallet.

Car.

Rucksack.

Of course, most people kept pictures on their phone
these days, and he had plenty of shots and videos of his
nieces and nephews there. But he still liked to hold
photographs in his hands. Feel the paper between his
fingers. For some reason, that made him feel like he
was closer when he was in some dark hole on the other
side of the world.

"And now I don't want to close my eyes," he said.

"I take it the nightmare shifted again."

He nodded.

"You know, you're talking yourself into some of this
by worrying about it all day."

"So, why are you having me write it down?" he
asked with a bit of a clipped tone. He'd become
obsessed by the dreams before she asked him to keep

a journal, and he wondered if that just made it all worse.

She raised the red liquid to her lips, taking a slow draw. "What are you afraid of most in this world?"

"What do you mean?"

"For example, I'm terrified of getting married, but I also don't want to spend the rest of my life alone. I fear I'll end up like one or the other of my parents, and I don't know which would be worse."

"I'm not afraid of much," he said, coating his heart with a thick layer of macho arrogance.

"We all have fears, and the ones that haunt our subconscious and affect our daily decision making are the ones that will keep us awake at night."

"Is that why you're awake tonight? Because your mother is close, and you don't want to be that person who has six husbands?"

"It's not the number that really scares me. I don't need a man like my mother does. But both parents are lonely for different reasons."

"Are you lonely?" he asked, honestly curious about how she felt about her life. He wanted to know what her hopes and dreams were.

"No. Not yet anyway. However, that is one of my biggest fears, and it comes to me in my dreams all the time. That said, you're deflecting this conversation."

"Hey, you're the one who keeps answering," he mused.

Her lips turned upward. "I do and that is a different

topic for another day. Tell me, what are you afraid of the most in life?"

"I used to think it was disappointing my mom. She gets this look on her face that just makes a man want to crawl in a hole and die."

"Try again."

"What? You don't believe me?" He raised his bad leg, bending at the knee and letting the boot sit across the cushion between them.

"I believe you want your mother to be happy, but if you were worried about disappointing her, you wouldn't sabotage every date she tries to fix you up on, and you'd be married by now."

He opened his mouth, but snapped it shut right quick. Damn woman had a point.

"Dig deeper, Dylan. Think about all the feelings you had when you wrote out your dreams as you remembered them."

He dropped his head back, closing his eyes, letting the images of the dreams and his emotions rise to the surface. "I'm really angry when I wake up."

"At who?"

"Myself because I'm hurting my family. Why would I do that?"

"You wouldn't," she said. The sofa shifted, and her tropical scent intensified. "Do you worry about what might happen when you're gone? If you die?"

He sucked in a breath. Nick had mentioned that one of the reasons he didn't think he could ever love again had been because of what dying does to the living.

Dylan had always thought Nick just didn't want to get hurt again, but his words made sense.

"I do, but I know my brothers and mother will survive without me."

"What about your brothers' wives? Their children?"

He raised his head, opening his eyes. She'd scooted to the middle of the sofa, her hand resting on the foam boot covering his bum leg.

"I'm not a big piece of their life, so not sure what you're getting at."

"The bigger your family gets, the more people there are to love, the more people there are to disappoint, leave behind, or die."

"But what does that have to do with my dreams?"

"You keep adding people to the nightmare, it could be you're associating the pain of losing your men to what it would feel like to lose your family, or what they would feel if they lost you, or it could be—"

"Huh. Interesting." It made sense, but he figured the simplicity of it was too easy. If it were that straightforward, he should be able to close his eyes and not have his heart rate sore to one hundred beats per minute. It shouldn't bother him to see a set of jumper cables and not remember feeling his brain ignite. This nightmare was more sophisticated than that.

But this was a start.

"I've treated many patients with PTSD, and while you definitely exhibit signs, I think these dreams are stemming from something other than your mission and lost men."

"What do you mean?"

"I would bet that when you write in the journal, it's all about your family, not your men." She held up her hand. "I'm not saying the lost souls aren't impacting you, because I know they are. I'm saying, this triggered something from your childhood you just haven't dealt with. A deep-seated fear you might not even know exists."

"I had a pretty easy childhood. Other than my father dying when I was a teenager, I come from a loving, tight family unit. My brothers and I have a unique bond. I wasn't bullied in school, nor was I ever a bully. I can't imagine that anything other than what I went through could be causing these nightmares."

"Oh, I'm sure they are the cause, but they aren't the effect."

"I really don't follow." He pinched the bridge of his nose. He'd seen other really good soldiers lose their careers to PTSD and nightmares, and he didn't want to be one of them, which was why he'd try like hell to make sense of what Kinsley told him.

She leaned closer, cupping the side of his face. "You know that experiencing the torture in your dreams and hearing your men suffer, isn't a nightmare. It's a reality that you are dealing with. If you weren't, we wouldn't be sitting on this sofa talking. This dream, the moment your family entered it, became something else. I think you're terrified you will die, leaving behind a family to suffer in a pain so great, there isn't anything that will fill the void, and at the same time, you're afraid that you won't leave behind a legacy."

He didn't mean to laugh but couldn't help it. "I don't want to cause my family any pain, but my job is dangerous, and considering what I just went through, I could very well die on the job, so what you just said, I don't buy."

She dropped her hand to her lap and let out a long breath. "I know you have a limited amount of time here and I'm rushing this process, but I think you've spent a lifetime trying to close the void your father left—"

"I'll admit, losing my father was traumatic, but my brothers and mother filled that void quite nicely."

"No. That's not what I mean. Your subconscious is telling you that taking every dangerous mission handed to you doesn't do the trick anymore. Teetering on life and death doesn't protect your heart from the suffering of losing someone you love, especially when you've never loved someone outside of your family so deeply it hurts." Staring at him with an arched brow, she sipped her wine.

He took a moment to collect his thoughts, which weren't too many because he couldn't wrap his brain around her analysis. It didn't compute. "Are you trying to tell me I'm having a recurring nightmare because I'm afraid I'll die alone?"

"I'm saying you're afraid you won't have anything to leave behind when you do die." She reached out, curling her fingers around the bottom of his T-shirt. "These scars are constant reminders of good men who died, and you will have them with you, as if they left a piece of them on you. You carry pictures of your family and talk about your nieces and nephews as extensions of your brothers' lives. Not yours. If anything, you keep them in this little box, protected from you and your world, as if you don't matter as much as they do." She tapped the center of his chest with her index finger. "And you said so before."

"I did not," he said with a furrowed brow, back-tracking the conversation.

"Right now, you don't see your life as mattering as much as all the men who died, your father, and even your brothers."

His CO once told him that if something made him really angry, then there was a layer of truth he needed to look at.

Dylan swallowed the rage boiling in his gut. "I'm not some guy on a death wish. Ramey was a huge adrenaline junkie and even he didn't push the envelope to the point he flirted with death."

"That's not the point."

"What is the point?" he said in a harsh tone. One he wished he could take back. He truly wasn't upset with her or her analysis of his dreams, but the idea she could be right made him want to volunteer for another mission.

Meaning, she was right.

"Tell me, are you and your brothers as tight as you once were?"

He drew his lips into a tight line. Being the baby,

he'd sometimes felt like he was one step behind his brothers. That said, he knew his brothers would always have his back.

If he asked.

He just never asked.

Not even when he needed them.

"All right," she said, tightening her ponytail. "Answer me this then. How many of the nine men were married? Fathers?"

"All married, four were fathers." He clenched his fists. "It should have been me," he whispered.

"Because you don't have a wife or children," she said matter-of-factly. "I think you're hurting your family in the dream because they all represent what you don't think you deserve."

"Now that is some crazy-ass bullshit." He put his glass on the coffee table. "No offense and I appreciate the time, but—"

"Don't finish that statement." She stood, patting his shoulder. "Go home. Get some sleep. Call me if you want to or need to. I'll leave my phone on all night."

"You're a good person, Kinsley, but you're wrong."

"I'll talk to you soon," she said with confidence as she held open the door. "I told my mother I had to work late tomorrow."

"And you don't?"

She laughed, shaking her head. "Want to go down to Palm Beach Gardens and get a drink at Topper's with me?"

"Sure."

"I'll text you when I'm done. You can Uber down, and I'll drive us home."

He leaned in and kissed her cheek. "Sweet dreams, Kinsley."

God, he hoped his dreams were filled with sunshine and unicorns.

8

_____

insley took the hottest shower she should could tolerate right after Dylan left. Her muscles ached, and her brain hurt, but not because of him.

She'd spent hours earlier in the day letting her mother cry on her shoulder, again. Knowing that in a few months, she'd find her 'soulmate.'

Again.

And that was too bad, because husband number six had seemed like a genuine keeper and he had really loved her mother.

But Kinsley could handle all that. What drove her mad was when her mother started babbling about calling Kinsley's dad. He'd answer and listen and then her mother would find someone else. It had been hell watching her mother break her dad's heart.

Over and over again.

Her father had learned, but he always took the phone call.

Always came running to her mother's side for moral support.

After towel-drying her hair, Kinsley put on a pair of shorts and a T-shirt, letting her thoughts wander back to Dylan.

She desperately wanted to help him understand that loving someone didn't make him responsible for their lives. He felt responsible for the men in his unit, which meant, no matter what happened on a mission, when it went bad, Dylan soaked it all in like an emotional sponge, always wishing it had been him who had died.

But when it went well, he never once considered he might be part of the success. No. He was just there, riding on the coattails of everyone else. He viewed his success as a byproduct of his brothers.

And his father.

That's where it began.

Whatever happened in that hospital room moments before his father died, changed Dylan forever.

She twisted her hair into a braid and headed for the kitchen. One more glass of wine. While pouring the rest of the bottle, she glanced out the window and gasped.

"Dylan?" she whispered, staring at him sprawled out on her beach chair. Tiptoeing to the front door, she peeked outside. "Dylan?" she repeated. "What are you doing?"

He rolled his head to the side. "Stargazing."

"On my porch?"

"I didn't want to go home just yet."

"Why didn't you text me or knock on the door?" She leaned against the doorjamb, her heart crumbling into a bunch of tiny pieces for the man with a heart of gold and a soul that needed some serious healing.

He dropped his feet to either side of the chair and patted the cushion.

She hesitated for only a couple of seconds and eased between his legs, facing him. She crisscrossed her legs and let out a long breath, staring into his ocean-colored eyes that called to her like her favorite ice cream.

"That's a big-ass glass of wine," he said, taking it from her hand and sipping.

"Figured I might as well finish the bottle."

"Afraid to go to sleep, too?" he asked.

"Not afraid, but I get insomnia, and tonight is one of those nights."

"Hence the massive amount of alcohol. This has to be half the bottle."

A pang of shame rolled across her stomach. Not the best way to handle the situation, but better than a sleeping pill. That shit made her nuts.

"Well, since I'm now sharing with you, I won't be drinking it all by myself."

"Why can't you sleep?" he asked in a that kind, caring voice that she suspected made all his men feel at ease. Dylan was the kind of man that people trusted to have their back. He had honor, humility, and a sense of duty that couldn't be taught.

"Do you want my clinical analysis of my problem? Or your average Joe version?" The only difference would be the language she used.

"How about the latter."

"My mother drives me fucking crazy, and my father is a wet noodle sometimes." She chugged the wine like it were grape juice. At least this time her father hadn't come running and was currently on a special assignment so he had no plans on making the trek from Orlando to Jupiter.

But he had listened to his ex-wife on the phone for over an hour.

Dylan snagged the glass after the third gulp. "You just called the man you want to fix my mom up with, a wet noodle," he said with a huge grin.

She laughed, shaking her head. "Why he sits and listens to my mom cry over other men, is beyond me."

"Why my mother hasn't dated once since my father died, is a concept that I can't fathom. I mean, after Nick's first wife died, she still pushed him to date, but never once went out herself, no matter how hard we pushed."

"It's shocking that men aren't pounding down her door. She's not only kind and loving, she's hot."

"Hey, that's my mother we're talking about." He winked. "But the apple doesn't fall far from the tree either."

"Conceited much?"

He lifted his hand, making the inch sign with his thumb and index finger. "Just a little." His smile faded. "Why do you let your mother get under your skin?"

"Because she's my mother and I love her, despite her crazy life. I remember when she and my dad split, before she met husband number three—"

"Wait, your dad wasn't number one?" Dylan asked, resting his hand on her bare knee.

She watched his thumb gently rub against her skin. A warm shiver glided from her legs to her brain, making her want things she had no business desiring.

Especially with a man like Dylan.

"Nope. Her first husband lasted three months. My dad, six years, and since then, the longest marriage only two years." Kinsley wanted to laugh at how easily Dylan kept the focus on her and her problems, avoiding his own. "My mom ends up having these emotional affairs, which is why her husbands keep leaving her, and I can always tell they are coming because she starts calling my dad. He used to fall for it, and I think the first time he hoped they'd get back together, for my sake, but they didn't. The worst part is she wants to all of a sudden be a mother, forgetting she left me at sixteen to run off and get married. My dad flipped out over that one, and I moved in with him."

"Wow. That's crazy." He tapped her knee.

"What's really nuts, is this time I didn't see it coming. She didn't call my dad until she showed up here and from what I can tell, there is no other guy she's conversing with, so I don't get it."

"Is that why you went into psychology? To fix your mom?"

She covered her mouth to keep from laughing so loud that she'd wake the neighbors. "I wanted to understand her, but subconsciously, you're probably right."

"The subconscious is a fucked-up thing." He reached out, twirling the ends of her braid with his fingers. "I was the last person to see my father alive."

She held her breath for a long moment.

"He spoke to me in his hospital bed."

"What did he say?" she asked softly.

"He told me he loved me. That he was proud of me. The usual things."

She held his forearm, rubbing gently. "Usual?"

"He told me not to be afraid. He knew he was dying, so he wanted me to know that we'd all be okay without him, but that we needed to take care of Mom."

"Your mom is one tough cookie."

"Yeah, she is." Dylan's fingers continued to fiddle with the ends of her hair. His gaze followed the movement of his hand.

"There is more, isn't there?" she asked.

"He had me promise I'd tell my brothers how much he loved them too." Dylan's Adam apple bobbed as he swallowed. The moon shined on his face, showing a gloss over his cool eyes. "During captivity on this last mission, when the torture would end, and my men were brought back into the holding cell, near death, they'd all say the same things."

"They'd want you to tell their families they loved them," she whispered. "How long were you in captivity?"

"Fifteen days," he said, squeezing his eyes shut. "They had already started torturing the Marines before we got there. They'd take two to three men at any given time then bring them back, broken and bloody. Five of them died in my arms, begging me to give messages to their loved ones, if I survived."

"Dylan." She cupped his face, leaning closer. "Look at me." She waited patiently as he blinked his eyes open.

"I called every man's family and gave their loved ones their dying words, and every time I did it, I could see and hear my mother cry and my brothers bite back their own tears as I told them I got to speak to Dad right before he died. My mom asked me if Dad had been in pain. My brothers asked if he was frightened, and all I could think about was how I saw him take his last breath and how I felt his heart stop beating under the palm of my hand. The man I knew and loved slipped from his body, and I couldn't get him back."

She kissed his forehead. "Those last few moments are a blessing and a curse."

"You're telling me." He wiped his eyes and adjusted her body so her head rested against his chest. His heart thumped against her ear. "Can I stay with you tonight?"

---

*D*ylan squeezed his eyes shut, holding the tears behind his lids so they didn't stream down his cheeks. He hadn't cried since his father died. Not even when he'd called his men's families. It wasn't that he didn't think men should cry, but he could never bring the emotions to the surface.

Both his mother and Kinsley had been right.

He stuffed every feeling he ever had, telling himself that this is how a proud man behaved. His father faced death with a smile on his face. Not that he wanted to die, but he accepted it. Nick said his first wife had done the same thing, and that had tormented Nick for many years.

But it wasn't just his father's death that woke Dylan up in the middle of the night.

"I don't know," Kinsley whispered. Her warm breath tickled his chest.

He kept his arms wrapped gently around her body, resting his chin over the top of her head, enjoying her way more than he ought to. He knew it was a lot to ask of someone who was essentially a stranger to spend the night, even if he didn't expect anything other than conversation, no matter how attracted he was to her.

"Your mom would worry if you didn't go home."

He chuckled. "I'm a grown man. I think I can stay out all night if I want."

"You know what I mean." She pushed from his chest, resting her hands on his shoulders. "She's already stressed—"

"It's nearly one in the morning, and I texted her a few hours ago that I was here, with you, and wasn't sure when I'd be home. She knows where to look for me if she gets worried."

"That's not the point, and you know it."

"Are you talking about all the sexual tension between us? Because I think I know how to behave like a gentleman. I promise to fend off all your advances." He'd never been good at humor like his brothers Logan and Ramey, and by the way Kinsley's nose crinkled, he figured this attempt hadn't gone over as planned.

Not to mention, he hoped to lighten up the conversation.

"You're really full of yourself, aren't you?"

"Are you denying there is something there?" That question had nothing to do with being funny and everything to do with how much he wanted to bury himself in her both emotionally and physically. He hadn't meant to open up that can of worms, but since he put it out there, he might as well find out her thoughts.

Thoughts?

Or was it her feelings?

Well, hell, maybe he was learning something.

She'd probably tell him that this was just another one of his many tricks to avoid his problems.

And she'd be partially right.

But he'd be lying to himself if he didn't admit feeling an intense, very real pull toward Kinsley. She was like no other woman he'd ever met. She made him want to push past his issues and move forward with his life.

She almost made him want to have a real relationship with a member of the opposite sex.

Sitting upright, she put some distance between them. "No. I won't deny that I'm attracted to you, but I'm doing my best to help you with your nightmares. Acting on that attraction wouldn't do you any favors."

"I beg to differ," he said as his lips tugged into a broad smile. "But what I want to know is if it would do you any favors?"

"Dylan, I need you to be serious and stop deflecting the issues with your charm." She stood, pulling over another chair, and sipped the wine.

Nothing like crashing and burning.

"You find me charming?" He winked.

She cocked her head and glared. "Why don't you want to go home? And don't say it's because you want to flirt with me. It might be true, but it's not the underlying reason."

He nodded. She deserved the truth. "I don't want to sleep in my childhood bedroom. Every time I climb between the sheets, all I see are my brothers and my dad. They are good memories, but it slowly turns fucked up the second I drift off."

"That makes sense," she said, resting her hand on his leg, handing him the glass of wine. "Have you been injured in other ops?"

"Not mortally. I've had a bullet graze me. Broken a leg and arm. But nothing like this."

"And you've been on missions where others have been killed," she said.

He nodded.

She flicked her braid behind her shoulders. "Did something else happen to you as a child? Something equally traumatic as losing your dad or your sister-in-law."

Dylan reached way back into the dark recesses of his mind. He hadn't talked about Colin, his best friend in first grade, in years. "The only thing I can think of is my friend who died of meningitis when I was seven." He remembered Colin had spent the night. He hadn't been feeling well when he woke up, and by that evening, he'd died.

"That's a lot to take in as a child." Kinsley slapped at her arm, missing the mosquito that had been buzzing around.

"Let's go inside."

Kinsley let out a long sigh. "This does not mean I have agreed to you spending the night."

"Understand." He collected the empty wine glass and followed her inside. While she got them a couple of waters, he sat on the far side of the sofa.

Kinsley sat next to him, tucking her feet under her nice, round ass. "How close were you and this little boy?"

"About as close as two seven-year-olds can be. After

the funeral, his parents gave me his Lego collection. My mom still has it."

"That's a sweet gesture."

Dylan nodded. "I never could bring myself to play with them. Every time I looked at them, all I could see and hear was his parents wailing in front of his casket."

"Did you ever think it should have been you?" She reached out, resting her hand on his thigh, squeezing gently.

"I wondered why it wasn't me. I wondered why I didn't get sick. I also worried the rest of my family could have gotten sick, I mean they wouldn't let me or my brothers back in school until we all had shots and taken oral pills to help prevent us from getting it."

"You always wonder why it wasn't you. Your friend. Your father. I bet you even took that on when Nick's first wife died."

Dylan closed his eyes, sucking in a deep breath. "I was supposed to be on the boat with them that day. I opted to do something else." The weight of death surrounded him like a snowstorm with blustering winds that created whiteouts. "I don't think I felt responsible, especially for my father's death. He was shot in the line of duty. That had nothing to do with me."

"Doesn't matter. None of these deaths are on you, not even the men you lost on this last mission, but do you see where I'm going with all this?"

Dylan blinked his eyes open. Kinsley had leaned forward. Her thick eyelashes flashed over her blue orbs like butterfly wings. She eased his aching heart and filled his mind with hopeful wishes. Thoughts he had never expected he'd ever consider. "I understand, but it doesn't account for my dreams."

"But it does." Kinsley cupped his face. "In your dreams, everyone you care about seems to be standing in line to be tortured. But your father, your brothers, they don't represent themselves, they are an adaptation of the torture you feel in your heart. The hurt you cause yourself when bad things happen to everyone else. The men that died brought all your emotions to the surface. Feelings you've never allowed yourself to express, going back to when your friend died."

He wanted to tell her that her assessment was full of shit.

Only it was spot on and he knew it. "Why don't I let myself feel things at the time they happen?" Tears welled in his eyes. A sob bubbled in his throat. He didn't want to cry. Not ever and certainly not in front of her. He remembered the second his father took his last breath, climbing up on the hospital bed. He had no idea how long he had lain there, hugging his father, bawling like a baby.

And it did nothing to help him through the pain of losing the man he admired the most. Every day since that day, a dark cloud seemed to hang over Dylan. It wasn't that bad things happened, because his life had been pretty damn good, but having to tell his brothers what their father had said, seeing their reaction, feeling their anguish, he shut down. It was all too much for his heart to bear.

Even Logan once told him that he needed to open up. When they'd all get together and discuss their missions, he'd seen all his brothers get teary-eyed, where Dylan either used the stance *I can't talk about that mission,* or *I don't want to dwell on it. Just learn from it.*

But what had he learned?

"I don't have an answer for that." Kinsley rubbed her thumbs across his cheeks.

He felt the moisture of the tears pouring out of his eyes.

"But if I had to guess, you didn't want to ever be the cause of anyone's pain. Anyone's tears. Anyone's utter sadness over anything and when you are forced to face it, you go back to the idea that it should have been you. That you have no legacy to leave behind, so no one will ever really miss you that much." Kinsley pressed her lips against his cheek. "You give only a little bit to your family, even though you're close, you still push them away. Your father's dying words of love and strength have stood with you, but not in the way I think he meant. You're the one who had to deliver those emotions to your brothers and you believed, in a weird way, that you caused them pain. That it was your fault. Just like you did when you called your men's families."

He grabbed ahold of Kinsley, pulling her tight to his chest, even though it hurt like hell. Desperation gripped his pounding heart. He half-expected to hear horrible howling vomit cries coming from his mouth, but instead, the tears simply and silently rolled down his cheeks.

Holding Kinsley as close as he could, he spread out on the sofa. All he wanted was her kindness. Her warmth. Her caring heart and soul.

No. He wanted so much more, but he knew tonight would not be the night.

9

*K*insley had her fair share of crying patients, but never had she let one fall asleep in her arms, on her sofa. Guilt tugged at her heart as she thought about how much she wanted to share a bed with Dylan. She shouldn't be thinking about sex. Her only thoughts should be on how to help Dylan continue letting his emotions out, coping with the losses in his life, and giving him the tools so he can go back to what he does best.

She let out a long sigh.

Exactly what he did for Delta Force was a mystery to her, but she knew it included activities that could potentially kill him.

Not to mention take him to faraway places on a regular basis.

She rested her hand on his chest. It rose and fell with each restful breath. Slipping from the sofa, she covered him with an afghan and headed toward her bedroom with a quick pit stop in the bathroom.

Before climbing into bed, she checked the time.

Three in the morning. Her alarm would be going off in a few hours. She had three clients, one meeting, and a ton of paperwork, but it was Friday, and that meant she'd have the weekend to catch up.

She groaned, shifting in bed, pulling the covers up to her chin. How could she have forgotten her mother was still in town, crying over her latest failed marriage? Kinsley's weekend would be filled with trying to talk her mother off the cliff AND keeping her from sitting at the bar, trying to attract eligible bachelors.

If she hadn't found one already.

Reaching toward the nightstand to shut off the lamp, she gasped, staring at Dylan standing in her doorway. The moon filtering in through her window glowed over his tall, broad body. His strong silhouette covered the space like a sexy cowboy strutting in from a long day wrangling horses. Not that she knew anything about cowboys or horses, but damn, Dylan had some serious sex appeal.

Even injured.

"You scared me," she whispered. "Did you have a bad—"

"No dreams. First time I woke up slightly peaceful since I was tortured."

She fluffed the pillow and lifted herself to a sitting position. For only a second, she questioned her decision to pull the covers back on the other side of the bed.

He inched closer. His lips curled into a soft smile.

"I want to make a few things clear," she said, needing to protect her heart and his as well. They each had their own issues regarding commitment, something neither one of them had ever really discussed, but she understood his and suspected he'd accept hers. "Your cognitive processing is getting better. I'm no neurologist, but over the course of this week, I've seen little to no signs of any problems. I believe you're going back to Delta Force the second you get the thumbs up."

He pulled his shirt over his head, tossing it on the floor in front of her closet. "I'll find out tomorrow if the doc thinks my brain is functioning properly. I feel confident that will be good news, which means, yes, as soon as my body is healed, I'm back to active duty."

She swallowed her own emotions, fighting the strong feelings that swelled deep in her soul. She and Dylan could never have more than a night or two in each other's arms. A relationship with him was destined to fail.

"What else do you want to clarify?" He rolled his jeans over his hips before sitting on the edge of the bed, fiddling with his removable cast. His back muscles flexed, but it was hard not to focus on the scars covering half his back. Tentatively, she reached out, but quickly retreated.

"I don't want a relationship with anyone right now.

I've got a lot of things going on, and I don't have room for a man, even one as sweet and kind as you," she said.

He tapped his chest. "Ouch, but I do understand. I'm not like my brothers. I don't want to get married, have kids, settle down. I like my life and other than this little blip in my psyche, I have no intention of changing anything about my life, but that doesn't mean I don't want to be with you, even if it's only for a short time."

Her eyes widened as he removed the rest of his clothes before putting his boot back on and climbing between the sheets, shamelessly naked.

"It's not that I don't care, because I do." He rested his head on his elbow, his other hand inching under her T-shirt. "I like you. You're kind, and sweet, and I feel comfortable with you. More so than I have with any other woman I've ever spent time with. However, I'm probably going to only be here until the day after the parade, and then back to Ft. Bragg, so, if you think a few nights of intense passion is a bad thing, I'll get dressed and leave now. No hard feelings."

"I wouldn't have invited you in my bed if I didn't want to spend the night with you."

He arched a brow. "Do I sense a but or another thing we need clarified?"

Laughing, she ran her hand gently across his chest, avoiding the raw scars that still had to cause him some pain. "I don't want to hurt you. You're still in a cast, and your wounds—"

He groaned, dropping his head to her chest. "And here I was feeling confident I could give you a fantastic evening, satisfying you until you sank into a deep sleep in my arms. Now I'm wondering if I'll even be able to perform."

She burst out laughing, which was a completely inappropriate response.

"I don't see the humor in that statement."

Sitting up, she yanked her shirt off, exposing her bare chest. Her nipples puckered in the cool air. She resisted the urge to cover them as he stared like a doe in headlights. "You can just lay there. I'll do most of the work."

Cupping her breast, rolling her nipple between his thumb and forefinger, he shook his head. "That doesn't work for me, but I think I'll have to pass on swinging from the chandelier." He winced when he tried to raise his upper body.

"Let me bring them to you," she murmured, shocked by her ability to tease, at the same time lifting her breast to his mouth, letting him take his fill.

He held her gaze as his tongue flicked over the hard nub, his free hand roaming up and down her back, tracing a line over her spine, slipping his fingers under the fabric of her shorts.

With every sharp inhale, her lungs burned with desire. As she exhaled, a moan got caught in her throat.

"Can we please get you out of these?" He tugged at the elastic.

"Gladly." Without wasting any time, she kicked off the rest of her clothes, while shoving the sheets to the foot of the bed. "I can't say I've ever made love to a man with a boot on one leg."

He laughed, though it wasn't a funny sound, more like a sarcastic grunt. "Or burns and scars all over his body."

Kneeling next to him, she raised her finger over his chest, scant centimeters from a scar. "Does it hurt if I touch?"

"More like itches at this point."

Tentatively, she grazed his tender body with her fingertips. The red skin felt tighter than the rest, but he showed no signs of pain. She leaned over, kissing each burn mark, and traced her finger across every scar. She couldn't fathom the physical and emotional pain he'd endured. She tried not to focus on it too much because it brought tears to her eyes, and this wasn't the time or place for that kind of emotion. This was all about healing.

And not just him.

His fingers threaded through her hair as she brought her lips to his. Their tongues rolled together like a roasted marshmallow melting chocolate over a graham cracker. His touch tender and sweet. Nothing desperate or rushed. Every movement had purpose. He explored her as if she were a fine piece of art, and she did the same. She wanted to know what every inch of his body felt like.

Tasted like.

How it smelled and how his muscles would react with different ways she brought him pleasure.

"It's been a long time since I've been with a woman," he whispered, pushing her to her back. He scooted down the bed.

"What constitutes a long time?"

"Over six months." His tongue glided up her inner thigh while his gaze captured hers, not letting it go.

Clutching the sheets in her hands, she prepared for what she hoped would last more than a few minutes. Not on his part, but on hers.

Her body ached and throbbed and she figured if his mouth touched her intimately, she'd cave, quivering before it even really began.

"But something tells me this is going to be like nothing I've ever experienced before and will be impossible to top, ever," he whispered as his lips kissed her hard, throbbing nub.

Dropping her head back, she held her breath for long moments before sucking in air, only to let it out in a guttural moan. He didn't rush, but he didn't leave any part of her untouched or undevoured. He made her feel like giving her pleasure made his all the sweeter.

Or that her satisfaction meant more to him than his own.

Either way, she wasn't going to second-guess her need to be pleased, or her selfish desire to take all he had to offer.

Her toes curled as she tried to fend off the rush that threatened. It felt like waves crashing into the sand, pulling her into the water, only to bring her back to the shore. It was a push and a pull that sent her body reeling.

She did everything she could she could to keep herself from letting go, but it came to no avail. "Dylan," she said in a panty breath, her legs closing around his head. Her hands digging into the bed. Her screams filling the room as the scent of sex engulfed her. He trembled for a good five minutes as he kissed, and prodded, and continued to make her body shiver like the aftershocks of an earthquake.

"God, I hope I can make you do that again," he murmured as he kissed his way up her stomach, shifting slightly as he gently kissed one nipple, then the other. "This position, though, is killing my ankle, mind being on top?"

She cupped his face. "Is that request really because of your ankle, or more of a personal preference?"

"I like sex in every position, so this would work just fine, but really, the angle kind of hurts my foot."

"Your honesty will get you whatever you want." Shamelessly, she rolled on top of him, straddling him, careful not to hit his foot, or bother too many of his wounds. Taking him slowly inside, she squeezed herself around his length.

He dug his fingers into her hips. His eyelids grew heavy as he moaned, tightening his body. "I won't last half as long as you did."

"Is that a challenge?"

"God, no. I want you to orgasm again more than I want to and good Lord, do I want to."

She lowered her hand, rubbing her fingers across her tight nub as she rocked gently over him, grinding slowly, then lifting up and down.

He stared up at her, his chest rising and falling in rapid succession. His body tensed in unison with hers. Their eyes locked on one another. She couldn't think of another time sex had been this powerful.

Intense.

Loving.

With that thought, her orgasm ripped through her like a raging river headed toward a steep waterfall. She clutched at his chest, calling out his name.

He pulled her close, kissing her lips, moaning deeply into her mouth as he lunged his hips upward, slamming his orgasm inside her.

Every inch of her skin tickled with delight. Her stomach quivered over and over again, and she wondered if it would ever stop.

As he slowed the motions of their bodies, she collapsed on top of his chest. His fingers danced up and down her spine as he kissed her cheek and neck, whispering how wonderful he thought she was and how amazing this night had been.

He might have even said thank you as she drifted off to sleep tucked neatly in his arms.

For the first time, she felt like she might have found home.

10

*K*insley didn't regret much in her life, and she sure as hell didn't regret sleeping with Dylan, but that didn't change the fact that he'd be walking out of her life in a week.

The morning sun had yet to fill the sky as Kinsley quietly slipped from her bed. Dylan lay blissfully asleep and if she wasn't mistaken, he had a smile on his face. In the few hours they had slept, not one single nightmare. She knew he wasn't cured, but he was on the mend. Understanding the source of one's anguish was a big step. Accepting it was huge, and Dylan had accepted it with every ounce of his being.

He wanted to understand and move past it, and that made her job easier.

Only it wasn't a job.

She stepped from her bedroom, not closing the door all the way since it would make a creaking noise.

She really didn't want to disturb him, though part of her still worried that he could have a horrible dream and wake up screaming.

Padding toward the kitchen, she started a pot of coffee and found her phone. Damn, only ten percent charged, but she did have a charger in her car and that should be enough to get through the day.

It buzzed with a text message.

Catherine: Sorry to bother you, but Dylan isn't answering his phone. Is he okay?

alk about awkward. How the hell did she answer that one?

insley: Yes. He's sleeping and since I don't believe he had a bad dream, I hate to wake him, but I will if you want me to.

Catherine: No. But can I come over? I'll bring coffee.

Kinsley: Brewing a pot now. I don't have too much time. I have to leave for work in an hour and a half.

o be totally honest, Kinsley could get ready for work in twenty minutes. Lucky for her, she didn't have to dry her hair, and if she was indeed having a bad hair day, she'd simply put it up. And what little makeup she wore, would take three minutes to apply. The longest part of her morning was sitting on the porch, enjoying the sunrise, or taking a stroll on the beach. That was the only reason she got up so early.

So, she absolutely had time for Catherine, regardless of how embarrassing it might be.

Kinsley grabbed her mug and poured the dark, hot liquid before racing out of the house. She glanced down at her attire before she stepped onto the porch. A pair of leggings and a T-shirt should be fine. Her hair, on the other hand, had to say, *look at me, I had mad sex last night with your son.*

The latter part of that thought made her cough.

She managed to situate herself in her favorite chair before Catherine arrived, dressed and ready for work.

Catherine was a natural beauty with her dark-blond hair, blue eyes, and the figure of a twenty-year-old. But it was her warm, loving personality that made her the kind of woman men wanted to be with and other ladies strived to be like.

"Good morning, dear," Catherine said as she sat in the chair next to Kinsley, sipping from her own mug. "So, Dylan slept without a nightmare?"

Kinsley nodded.

"I take it he's really confided in you what's been going on in his head."

Kinsley never liked brushing people off, and even though Dylan wasn't a client, it wasn't her place to tell his mother anything. "We've talked, but I can't break his confidence in trusting me. Can we leave it at that?"

"Can I at least ask what you think of his progress? If he'll be able to go back to Delta Force the same man?"

Dylan would never be the same, not after what he experienced in the field, but her professional opinion was that he'd be able to go back and perform his duties to the best of his abilities, which she suspected were better than most. While she couldn't be certain with their short time together, she believed the reason his nightmares haunted him so much was that he felt responsible for everyone, including his brothers and their families. She wasn't sure if he would ever be able to let some of that go, but he did know he couldn't protect everyone all the time.

"Catherine, I told you at the start, that anything he has told me, or my professional opinion, would be between me and him."

"I can accept that," Catherine said with a nod. "He's my baby boy, and I worry so much about him. Not just because of his job. I was married to a cop. I've had three other sons have dangerous jobs. Hell, even with the Aegis Network, their jobs still can be risky, but Dylan has always been slightly withdrawn. Always hiding inside himself, never opening himself up to others. To a relationship. To love. Hell, even Ramey, the one who was a womanizing asshole for half his life, found the love of a good woman and mended his restless soul. Sometimes I think somewhere along the line, we broke Dylan's."

"He's not broken. Not like that," Kinsley said. "He's capable of love. Actually, he loves very deeply, he just needs his work. That's who he is. Trust me when I say, he'll get through this part of the healing process."

"That's kind of what I'm afraid of." Catherine set her mug on the table. "Logan, my oldest, was always so put together. He had goals, and he did what he needed to make them happen, even if that meant leaving behind the only woman he could ever love. It took him awhile to settle that restless heart of his, but he did. Nick, oh that one." Catherine clutched her heart. "He fell in love so hard and fast, he quit school, became a cop, and settled in for what he thought would be an easy life. When Joanne died, it shattered his hold on what he held dear. He ran off and followed Logan's path in the military. For years, I worried more about him than I did about Dylan, only I knew deep in my soul, Nick would find love again. It's who he is."

"All your boys are good men. It's a testament to their mother."

"Thank you," Catherine said. "Ramey doesn't talk about it ever, but he too had his heart broken. Different than Nick, but it changed him, and that's when women became people he shared a bed with. That was until Tequila walked into his life and turned it upside down, for the better."

"Not everyone is meant to be married. To be in a lifelong relationship."

Catherine let out a long sigh. "I can actually understand that. Since my Michael died, I have only dated a few times. I haven't been with another man in years, and I really don't have much of a desire to, but I at least experienced what that kind of love is like and as I always told Nick, it's better to have loved and lost than never know what that feeling is like."

"And you want Dylan to love someone, if only to know how it feels?" It wasn't really a question, but she posed it as one.

"Yes. I do."

Kinsley shifted so she could make eye contact. "My mother has been married six times, and I can tell you with each husband, she has loved them with all her heart and soul, but she doesn't know how to stay in love. She doesn't know what it takes to make it work. That doesn't make her bad, or broken, it's just who she is. Dylan loves his work. He loves his men like family, which is why this last mission was so hard on him. Being with a woman, falling in love that way, might not be what is best for him."

"What about for you? What is best for you?" Catherine asked with a scowl.

"I'm not the woman for Dylan, if that is where this is going." Kinsley held up her hand when Catherine opened her mouth in protest. "I do care about him. I let him stay here last night because I care more about him than I should. If there were a man I could fall for, it would be someone like him. But, Catherine, I have my own set of issues and I don't want to hurt your feelings, but Dylan and I aren't made for each other. We are simply two people who came together during a difficult time and helped each other. I think we'll always be friends, but don't push me on him. Don't push anyone on him. If he's going to fall in love and be with a woman, it will be on his terms."

Catherine tucked her hair behind her ears. "I'm not pushing either one of you into each other's arms. You both did that all on your own. All I'm asking of you now, and I'll ask my son the same thing when I see him, is to be honest with how you feel about one another. And how you really feel about the prospect of spending the rest of your life wondering if the right one got away."

Kinsley blinked, processing the same information her mother would toss out every time she walked down the aisle.

"I'm sorry," Catherine said. "That really isn't where I meant this conversation to go, only that I see you and my son together, and I know there is something there, even if you don't see it yet, or feel it, or are fighting it. My only wish is that the two of you take the opportunity to explore what might be."

Kinsley didn't want to be rude, but she felt it imperative to be frank. "Dylan and I both understand each other, and I'd be lying if I said I didn't find him attractive and didn't really enjoy his company. I think he feels the same about me, but neither of us wants to go down that road."

"I respect that," Catherine said with a grin. "But I

think you're both scared. I've seen it in my other boys, and I know Dylan." Catherine raised her hand. "That's all I'm going to say, and you need not say another word. I won't push. I won't pry. I will only say, from the bottom of my heart, thank you for helping my son."

A long silence filled the morning air, but a million thoughts plagued Kinsley's mind. Waking up in Dylan's arms had been nothing like she had ever experienced. It brought her joy and made her want to do it all over again. Most men she just wanted out of her house before they even fell asleep.

But Dylan made her want things she had no idea actually existed.

"Good morning, Mom. Kinsley."

Kinsley gasped, spilling her hot coffee down the front of her shirt. "Shit," she mumbled. "Dylan, you scared the crap out of me."

"Sorry," he said, leaning against the side of the house, raising his own mug to his lips and blowing on the scalding liquid with a wicked smile. "What are you two ladies up to this fine morning?"

"I was just getting ready to say goodbye and head to work." Catherine rose, giving her son a big hug and kiss on the cheek. "Dinner tonight? The three of us?"

"I'm game," Dylan said.

"I'm sorry, but I have plans with my mother." Kinsley glanced away, not wanting to see the hurt she might have put in Catherine's or even Dylan's eyes.

"Bring her. The more the merrier," Catherine said.

Before Kinsley could protest anymore, Catherine

had disappeared around the corner and into her own trailer.

---

*D*ylan rinsed his mug out in Kinsley's sink. He'd heard way too much of that conversation, and most of it settled in the pit of his stomach, sloshing around as if he'd just been on a twirling carnival ride. He wasn't sure what was worse, listening to his mother tell the woman he'd just slept with that she had deeper feelings than she was willing to admit, or hearing Kinsley say there was no hope for them as a couple at all.

The latter made him want to run off to Ft. Bragg on the next bus.

But why?

The answer to that question made his hands shake, and he dropped the mug. Thankfully, it didn't break.

Did he really want to be in a real relationship? Have someone to write home to? A picture to bring in his wallet of his girl, not all his nieces and nephews?

He shook his head as he wiped his hands dry, turning to lean his ass against the sink. No. He didn't want any of that. He didn't want anyone to worry about him. It was hard enough to know how much his mother did and even though his brothers understood, and they too had dangerous jobs, they had their concerns about Dylan's.

Problem was, he wanted Kinsley.

Not for one night. Or two. Or even three.

Fuck.

No way was he falling in love and the sooner he left town, the better off they'd both be. God, he was a dick. He used her, and now he was going to run away like a childish boy.

The smell of coconut mixed with the steam of a hot shower filled his nose as Kinsley waltzed out of the bathroom with her hair up in a towel, wearing a cute, little, white tank top and black slacks.

"Can I make you some breakfast?" What the fuck was he doing? First, he was in her house, so what right did he have to cook anything? And second, why was he still in her house?

"No, but thank you, that's very sweet."

He shrugged. "Every once in a while, I surprise myself."

"I've got to finish getting ready for work and isn't your cognitive appointment in a couple of hours?" She took a few steps closer, removing the towel, and shaking out her long, dark hair.

His breath hitched. It wasn't her beauty that made him gasp for air, but everything about who she was as a woman. The way she carried her confidence with humility made him want to be a better man.

Transfer…something or other. Whatever you called it when a patient fell for his therapist. That's what he was suffering from.

"Yeah. I should probably get going," he said.

She tossed the towel toward her bedroom, inching

ever closer with the sexiest smile he'd ever seen. Her hands slid up his chest, resting on his shoulders. "I didn't get to ask. How are you feeling this morning?"

"Restful," he admitted. His hands disobeyed his mind and circled around her waist. "I don't remember having any dreams." That was a lie. He had a dream of her sitting on the beach and she was crying, and he'd put those tears on her pretty face. When he'd woken up in her bed alone, his heart tightened. He had no desire to hurt her, and he feared he would. "I need to tell you something."

"If you're going to rehash that this is a temporary thing because you're leaving after the parade next Friday, then I'm going to stop you right there. I told you last night, I'm not in the market for a long-term relationship." She raised up on her tiptoes and kissed his lips gently.

"Then we're on the same page," he whispered.

"Good. Will you text me with what the doctor says?"

He nodded, swallowing.

Hard.

"Are you going to join my mother and I?" he asked.

"I have to check in on my mother, and I'd prefer to do that alone. Maybe drinks around nine? We can meet here, or maybe across the street."

"Here." He pulled her to his chest, brushing his lips over hers in a tender, but meaningful kiss. She was willing to have a fling, and so was he. "Just the two of us."

Problem solved.

"I'll see you tonight." He stepped back and pulled out his cell phone as it vibrated. He glanced at it. "My brother Ramey, I better get it." He kissed her forehead and turned on his heels, hobbling out her front door. His muscles ached, and he tried not to flinch. Last evening's activities caused him more pain than he'd ever admit to himself, much less anyone else.

"What's up, bro?" he asked as he tapped the button, waving to his mother who pulled out of the driveway. He was happy to see her go. Not because he didn't enjoy spending time with her, but he just didn't want a lecture on how to treat a lady, which would lead to how he should get married and give her even more Sarich grandbabies, because five wasn't enough.

"How are you feeling?" Ramey asked.

"I'm doing much better other than the ankle is still killing me," he said, limping up his front porch. "I see the neurologist this morning, so if all goes well, I'm heading back to Bragg next Saturday or Sunday."

"So, you're definitely going through with the parade?"

"Yeah. Since I'm getting two medals, if I bailed it would break Mom's heart, and I just can't do that to her even though I don't deserve them. Plus, General Maxwell is presenting them to me."

"He called. He wants me, Nick, and Logan involved. And Dylan, you're very deserving of them. I don't know what happened over there, but I do know you,"

Ramey's voice shook with emotion. "You're a true hero."

Dylan blinked his eyes. The screams of his men had subsided, the images subdued, but the pain in his heart would never mend. "I don't feel like one."

"Heroes never do," Ramey said, letting out a long breath. "I called to tell you that me, Tequila, and Kayla are coming on Wednesday. Everyone else is still coming on Thursday. I hope it's okay if we stay at Mom's. I know it's a lot—"

"It's fine. Mom will love it. But why are you coming early?"

"Tequila is pregnant, and we wanted to tell Mom alone. No one else knows, so don't blow it. But I also wanted to make sure it was okay we tell the family after the parade. We don't want to take away from your day."

"Congratulations." Dylan smiled, and his heart swelled with love. It was a weird sensation to be utterly thrilled about a new addition to the family. His brothers were his world, and so were their children. Part of him wished he wanted a little rug rat. "And please, take the focus off me. Make the entire thing about you and new babies. I'm begging."

"Consider it done," Ramey said. "I'll see you Wednesday around seven. I'll text Mom and let her know we're coming."

"See you then." Dylan slipped his phone into his back pocket. An engine revved.

Kinsley waved as she drove past.

He smiled, tapping his finger against his chest. He knew his life had changed when he woke up in the hospital in Germany. He expected it would after what he'd been through.

He had no idea spending a week with Kinsley would flip him upside down.

11

*D*ylan sat in the waiting room trying to keep his leg from rattling the floor as his knee bounced nervously. The tests were easy enough, though he did feel a little foggy in the brain, but his balance tests he'd had no problems with. That had to be a good sign. They'd also had him go down for x-rays and of course, the technician said absolutely nothing.

The door on the other side of the room flung open. "Come on in," Dr. Reese said. He was a short, bald man, who had to be close to fifty. He came highly recommended by many people, but especially by the Vanderlins who had used him when their son had been in an accident and had a brain injury.

But the most important reason he came to Dr. Reese was that he was still in the Army Reserves and on the list of approved doctors.

Dylan stood, his ankle still throbbing from last night. How sex could have affected his broken bone while still in its boot he had no idea, but it ached, and he limped more than usual. He understood why his ribs were sore, but not his foot.

He also understood why his mind had been scattered all day. He hoped it hadn't affected his test taking abilities because he needed out of Jupiter. Didn't matter that Kinsley said she didn't want a relationship, which he absolutely believed.

The problem was he had started imagining things with her that he'd never considered.

Ever.

"Take a seat." Dr. Reese sat behind a big desk in front of a built-in bookcase with dozens of thick books and a few pictures of what Dylan assumed were his family. "I've read everything in your file that the Army sent over. I can only imagine what was redacted and what really happened over there."

"It was a difficult deployment," Dylan said, knowing that much of the torture he and his men endured was kept from the public. As was their actual location, along with the details of the mission. The world thought they'd been flying over a known Taliban compound to rescue three Marines who had been missing when they were shot down. That part was true.

"I think it's amazing that you are alive, and that's not based on reading this," he said, holding up a thick folder. "I treated a few soldiers who had been tortured when I spent a year over there and, son, you endured more than most."

Dylan nodded. "I don't want to focus on that. I want

to know if I'm going to be able to go back and do my job. Delta Force is everything to me."

Kinsley could mean something to me.

He blinked, pushing that thought to a spot in his brain that he hoped would help it disappear into the abyss of a faint memory of feeling her body against his.

"Then I've got some good news for you. Your mind appears to be as sharp as a tack. I see no cognitive issues at all. No swelling in the brain anymore. I'll send my report in, but you do know you'll need to do all this again in a month, plus take a fitness test."

Dylan's mouth curled into a small smile. It was hard not to be excited about the prospect of being back in the field.

A tug at his heart lulled him back to Kinsley. He remembered a conversation he had with Ramey about why he couldn't re-enlist after meeting Tequila, and it had nothing to do with being deployed. She'd been in the Air Force and knew exactly what life with a military man would be like, and she didn't once tell him she wanted him to leave. She actually encouraged him to stay.

But the Aegis Network gave him the kind of job that allowed the adrenaline he still craved while having a family at the same time, without having to say goodbye to the woman who meant more to him than life itself for any real length of time.

Fuck.

Fuck.

Double fuck.

No way was he falling in love. He didn't love women. He liked them.

A whole lot.

But him?

In love with Kinsley?

"Dylan?" Dr. Reese said. "Did you hear me?"

Dylan shook his head. "Sorry, my mind wandered to this weekend and my being bombarded by my brothers and their brood of babies."

"I've met your oldest brother, Logan, a few times. Good man."

"He's the best," Dylan said. "They all are."

Dr. Reese nodded. "Anyway, as I was saying, I still want you to work on those balance exercises, brain teasers, and anything that will sharpen your memory and your attention span."

"Will do," Dylan said, standing with his hand stretched out.

"I know I've said it before, but thank you for your service."

"Yours as well." Dylan hobbled out of the office with his head held high. A heavy weight had been lifted off his shoulders just knowing that he had the faculties to do his job. However, he'd be lying if he wasn't worried about passing a physical. His ankle was in bad shape. He'd had emergency surgery before he'd even woken up in the hospital, and they mentioned he might need another one. The physical therapist said his muscles were strong, but the bones in the ankle, based on the x-ray, were about as bad as a break could be.

Perhaps a career in the Army wasn't at jeopardy, but his role in Delta Force very well could be.

He stepped out into the hot Florida heat and stared at the bright-blue sky. While the concern over his body was real, he should be thrilled about what Dr. Reese had said about his brain injury. It didn't matter that he'd only had one night without a nightmare, he believed what Kinsley had said about why he was hurting his family in his dreams. It didn't haunt his daily thoughts like it had yesterday. He knew he still had some work to do, and when he got to Ft. Bragg, he damn well would be scheduling a few sessions with the psychiatrist on base.

Kinsley had given him the courage to continue that discussion.

With a shaky hand, he pulled open the Jeep door and climbed in.

He should be happier about leaving next weekend. Not that he was ever thrilled about leaving his mother. He loved his mother and worried about her, but his brothers all lived so close, and they checked in on her all the time.

Something was holding him back and that something came in the form of a sexy, sweet, kind, and amazing woman named Kinsley.

"*I*t would be nice if you paid attention to your mother and not your phone."

Kinsley quickly finished her text back to Dylan, letting him know she'd do her best to make it back to her place by nine, but it was already eight thirty, and even though it was only a five-minute walk, at the rate her mother was babbling, it might be another hour before she could end the insanity that was her mother's venting.

And insistent eyelash-batting with the older gentleman at the end of the bar.

She went from biting back tears to a flirty smile faster than a bee sting.

And oddly, all of it was real.

"Sorry, Mom. But I told you I was meeting a friend in a little while, and I just wanted him to know—"

"Him? As in a man, him?" her mother's screech echoed across the cool ocean air at the outside bar at the Sun and Sand Jupiter Spa and Resort. All heads turned for one second toward their table.

"You did not say your friend was of the man persuasion. Tell me all about him. Who is he? What does he do? How handsome is he?" Her mother leaned in and winked. "Is he good in the sack?"

"Mother. Stop it." Kinsley did her best not to blush. Her mother had never had a filter, and when she was thirteen and needed to get tampons for the first time, her mother's free spirit made it easy to talk to her, but other than that, it was nothing short of embarrassing.

"Dylan is a friend, nothing more, nothing less."

"So, he has a name." Her mother took her fruity drink, twirling the little umbrella around before taking another sip, glancing over her shoulder. No doubt to make sure her new interest was still nursing his beer. "Could he be more than a friend?"

"No, Mom. He's my neighbor's son, and he'll be heading back—"

"As in the young soldier who was shot down a month ago and nearly died? I read about him in the papers. He's getting the Medal of Honor and the Purple Heart. I even heard that some big wig five-star general is coming to present it as well as the governor and a couple of senators."

Thank God her mother would never meet—

"Hey there," Dylan's voice rang out in her ears like a doorbell.

"Dylan?" she whispered, but not soft enough.

"Oh my God," her mother exclaimed, jumping from her seat. "Thank you for your service, and I'm so sorry for what happened to you, but I'm so happy you will be honored this Fourth of July."

"Thank you." Dylan pulled up a stool and sat down next to Kinsley, giving her a kiss on the cheek.

Wonderful.

"I hope I'm not interrupting, but I hadn't eaten, and if I said something to my mother, she would have cooked me a five-course meal, so I thought I'd head here and have a burger and fries. She says hello, by the way." He waved the waitress over and ordered his meal, along with Vodka soda.

"Your ears must have been ringing because my daughter was just talking about you, only now she's being rude. Let me introduce myself, I'm Robin." Her mother reached across the table with an outstretched hand.

Only she didn't expect a handshake, but a kiss.

And Dylan certainly didn't disappoint.

"I hope Kinsley was saying nice things about me."

"Well, we barely got started," her mother said with a bigger smile than necessary. "My daughter says you're just friends, but I can tell when a man is smitten."

Dylan took a sip of his drink and then choked. "We are good friends," he said, giving Kinsley an odd look with an arched brow and a crinkled forehead. "How long will you be staying in Jupiter?" he asked, changing the subject.

Thankfully.

"I don't know," her mother let out a long sigh, once again glancing over her shoulder. "I'd like to see the parade, but after that I fear I will have to head back to New Jersey to take care of some things."

"Well, I can make sure you have a ticket to the presentation. It won't be near Kinsley, since she's sitting with my family. But I can get you into the seated area if you like."

"Oh, yes. That would be wonderful. Thank you so much," her mother said, gushing.

"I see that gentleman over there is giving you some serious eyes," Dylan said.

Oh, dear Lord. He was going to push her in that man's direction. Hell, who was Kinsley kidding, her mother didn't need a push. She was going to find another man. Whether it be silver eyes over there, or someone else. And Dylan was doing her a solid by giving her mother permission to walk away from the table.

But would she?

And did Kinsley really want her mother to move on to husband number seven?

Well, hell. Being married made her mother happy in a weird way, even if they never lasted.

"I guess my daughter didn't tell you, but my husband and I are splitting, so I'm not interested in jumping into another relationship. That said, I should leave you two lovebirds alone."

"Mom, I told you—"

"Good night, darling. I love you." Her mother kissed her forehead as she stood. "And I'd love those tickets, even though it won't be near my daughter."

"I'll make sure you get them and if something changes in the family section, I'll let Kinsley know."

Her mother hugged Dylan as if she'd known him his entire life. She looked one last time at the man at the end of the bar before heading toward the doors that led to the lobby. The man soon followed.

"You don't have to give her tickets."

"It's not a big deal," Dylan said, sipping his drink.

"I didn't know I was expected to sit with your family."

He let out a long breath. "That wasn't the best way to ask you, but it would mean a lot to me and my mom. And I didn't mean to be rude with your mother, but I wasn't sure if you wanted her sitting with you."

"God, you're so sweet," she said, reaching over, resting her hand on his and kissing his cheek. "Thanks for coming and understanding that I love my mother, but sometimes need a break from her."

"Hey, I've got the best mom in the world, and I love her more than anything, but there are times I just need to walk away, like tonight."

"What do you mean? Did something happen?" Kinsley couldn't imagine anything coming between Catherine and her boys.

"Do you want the truth?" he asked as the waitress placed a plate of food in front of him. He wasted no time digging in, dunking a French fry in a wad of ketchup and popping it into his mouth.

"Should I be afraid of the truth?"

He nodded.

"Well, it can't be worse than knowing that my mother is probably going to sleep with that man tonight."

"My brothers and I once thought we'd love for our mother to have a man in her life, but then we all got weirded out about the idea of her having sex."

"If my mother knew we had sex, she'd be giving you tips on how to please a woman."

Dylan coughed, spitting out half his burger. "I don't think I could handle that conversation."

Kinsley stole a couple of fries, letting out a nervous laugh. "We got sidetracked. What happened with your mom?"

"I told her I was going to Ft. Bragg the day after the ceremony. I expected her to be upset that I wasn't staying longer, but I didn't expect her to give me a big old lecture about you and how I was an asshole when it came to women. She said some things I have never heard come out of her mouth, and she's kind of right."

"You're not a jerk when it comes to me. We both have been honest and after you leave, she'll see I'm not heartbroken over it." She hoped he didn't notice how she stumbled over the last few words. And it will be difficult for her not to be sad, but she wasn't going to let anyone see it.

Now, who was stuffing their feelings?

"Not that I want you to feel bad or anything, but I really do like you. More than I should." He wiped his face with his napkin and tossed it on the plate, leaning back in his chair. "If there were ever a woman I'd want to try having any kind of a relationship with, it would be you."

Her heart pounded in her chest, smacking against her ribs, making it hard to breathe.

"But my way of life isn't made for sharing. Last year, I was deployed all but two months and most of those days were spent either debriefing or preparing. I see my family only—"

"You don't have to explain it to me," she said as she took his hand. "I'd be lying if I told you I didn't have some kind of feelings for you, but you're leaving. I know that, and I'm still not interested in a long-term commitment. Not even with someone I like as much as I like you."

He waved the waitress down, giving her his credit card. While he signed the check, she took a moment to collect her thoughts, hoping to slow her raging pulse.

There was only one thing she was afraid of, and that was ending up like her parents. Yet, if she never took a risk, she'd be just like her dad. Or like Catherine. Alone. Perhaps happy, but alone.

Or she'd be like her mother. Never alone, always on a roller coaster, though, perhaps happy at times. The thing was, after spending this week with Dylan, she craved a partner in life.

And she wanted it to be Dylan.

"Come on, let's go. I drove, because my ankle is killing me." He rested his hand on the small of her back. They walked silently through the dark parking lot. Small lamppost lights lit the way down the path. The nearly full moon cast a white glow over them. "This might get me slapped, but are we going to spend the rest of my time here with each other, or are we going to part friends now?" He pulled open the Jeep door.

She paused, leaning against the truck, raising her

hand to touch the side of his face, which was still slightly bruised, but his scar wasn't as raised anymore. "I'm being selfish and reckless, but I'd like to spend time with you."

"*No!* Stop!"

Kinsley jumped as Dylan tossed and turned. She rubbed the hair from her face, just as he yelled, "Please, don't go!"

So much for sex taking care of his bad dreams. Not that it was a known or even good treatment plan, but it did take his mind off things for a bit.

"Dylan," she whispered, rubbing his arm gently. "Wake up."

He bolted to a sitting position, and his arms thrashed about, pushing her to the side as she tumbled off the bed, her ass landing on the floor with a loud and painful thud.

"Fuck. Kinsley, are you okay?" He groaned as he leaned over, stretching his hand out in an offer to help.

She glanced up at him. His lips pursed tight, indicating pain. Perspiration beaded across his forehead. "Sit back and relax. I'll get us some water."

He nodded.

Pushing herself off the floor, she waited to rub her butt until after she made it to the kitchen. The floor rattled under her feet. She whipped around and gasped. "Jesus, Dylan. Don't sneak up on me like that."

"Sorry. But I want to make sure you weren't hurt and to apologize for knocking you off the bed. I can't say I've ever done that before."

Patting his chest, she breezed past him and sat on the sofa. "It's okay."

"It's almost six in the morning, shall I just make a pot of coffee?"

"Yes, please, and while you do, you can start telling me about your dream. Was it the same as the last time?" Horrible to bait him like that, and she told herself that she was helping him by making sure he was honest.

Only that wasn't the truth.

He shook his head, letting out a long breath. "It went back to me being in a separate room, listening to them torture my men. Same dream I had in the hospital."

"You're lying." She could have gone easier on him, but then she'd be a shitty friend and that was one thing she prided herself on, her loyalty and honesty with her friends.

And Dylan was indeed a friend.

That was her story and she was sticking to it.

"Why would you say that?" He poured the water into the pot and flipped the switch. Leaning against the counter, he folded his arms in a defensive and closed position.

"Because you talked in your sleep."

He scowled. "What did I say?"

"No. Stop. Please don't go," she repeated his words.

Rubbing his temples, he turned away. "I've made an appointment to see the psychiatrist on base. I know I need to discuss the things that are swirling around in my subconscious before I go back in the field. You showed me how important that is. Thank you."

"Well, that sounded like a kiss-off," she said with a little more snap in her words than she wanted him to hear. He didn't need to know how much it hurt her feelings that he was closing himself off from her. Shutting himself down.

Basically, emotionally checking out, which is what they had agreed to in a weird way.

A week of sex.

And sex didn't equal an emotional attachment.

Only she had that too.

"I don't mean it to." He scratched the back of his head, still turned away, holding a coffee mug in his other hand, as if that would make it percolate any faster. "But I don't want to talk about it."

"All right," she ground out. She had no right to be mad.

"What are we doing?" He slammed the mug on the counter and turned. His eyes filled with the same anguish as the day she'd first met him. His jawline tight as if he were ready to explode.

"Excuse me?" She glared.

"You don't want a relat—"

"We had this discussion last night. Why is it bothering you now?"

"Because you deserve better. You deserve someone to love you and take care of you. Someone you can love back." The lines on his forehead crinkled, and he let out a long breath. She knew him well enough to know he was grappling with emotions he didn't want to deal with.

But she wasn't sure what they were.

"I don't need anyone to take care me, thank you very much. And I'm a grown woman capable of making my own decisions. It's not like neither one of us hasn't had a fling or a one-night stand before."

"That is a true statement," he mumbled as he hobbled back to the bedroom. He returned a few minutes later wearing his shirt and carrying his shoes. "I think it's best if we part friends now."

"Wow. Whatever was in that dream certainly spooked you. Was it about me?" Oh boy, did she know that was a passive-aggressive move on her part. One, fishing for information on how he might be feeling about her, and in the same breath, telling him she didn't care.

Talk about being an asshole.

He laughed, but it was more of a sarcastic sound. "Mighty egotistical of you, Doc. But if you must know. I dreamt about the day my father died. I was standing at the front door, and he was leaving for work. I just didn't want him to go as if I could stop him somehow."

"Jesus." She bolted from the sofa, racing across the room. "I'm sorry. I shouldn't have—"

He held up his hand. "But you did, though that's not the point."

"What is then?" She held her breath, staring at him, waiting for an answer.

"We just can't do this anymore. I need to focus on getting back in shape, and I'm sure you'll easily find another man to have a fling with while helping him solve whatever—"

"Get the fuck out, now." She pointed to the door. "And don't come back."

He nodded and left.

The second the door clicked shut, she let the tears fall. They weren't just for her and her hurt feelings over the harsh words Dylan had said.

But for him because he was never going to allow any emotions to surface. He'd work though what happened in the field by shoving them so far down with all the other shitty things he's had to deal with.

She glanced out the window. Dylan wasn't anywhere to be seen.

If he could only open that big heart of his, he'd have everything he could ever imagine and damn it, she wanted him to imagine her.

*D*ylan lay on the sofa, the boot he normally wore tossed aside while he iced his ankle. At least now he could move it, but the fucker hurt like hell.

But not as much as his heart.

Lying, unfortunately, had come easy to him most of his life, but especially in his work with Delta Force, so telling Kinsley that dream wasn't about her, and then making one up, well, easy as pie.

Dealing with the consequences of that lie, well, that was entirely something else.

Since then, he'd woken up three times to dreams about his men being tortured and dying. Their cries still echoed in his brain. But the dreams were fainter. And he was no longer killing his father, only his father did show up, as did his brothers, just standing off in the distance, as if they were waiting for him to come home. In the dream, he thought he'd heard his mother call that supper was ready.

Those dreams didn't haunt him anymore. They disturbed him and made it difficult for him to fall asleep, but what had woken him up this morning was the vision of Kinsley running down the beach. Running from him. Leaving him behind in a dark tunnel of nothingness. What the hell did that mean?

He tossed a tennis ball in the air with one hand, catching it with the other. He had no idea how long he'd been doing it, but the sun had been up for at least an hour.

"Oh, hey there," his mother said as she stepped into the kitchen. "I thought you stayed over at Kinsley's last night."

"I did, but you're right, Mom, I'm an asshole and I did the right thing, but in a really bad way."

"I see." Her mother pulled a couple of diet sodas from the fridge before sitting down on the end of the sofa, putting his leg in her lap, handing him a can. "I take it that means you ended whatever was brewing between the two of you."

"Nothing was brewing. Neither one of us has room in our lives for romance, and neither one of us wants it either."

"Then why are you sitting here sulking?"

"I'm not." He swigged his soda, letting the bubbles tickle his throat. "I'm icing my foot."

"Whenever you were upset over something, you'd lay somewhere tossing a damn ball up and down. So, what's going on?" His mother didn't let things go easily. "How mean were you to Kinsley?"

"She gave as good as I did, so let's just say we both weren't playing nice in the sandbox."

"Well, I can't believe I'm going to say this, but if neither of you have any desire to try to make this work, then it's best to end it now."

"Wait a minute. You're not going to push me about getting married and having kids and all that shit? You used to tell me you thought this neighbor was perfect for me. Hell, last night, you were telling me I needed to really examine my feelings when it came to Kinsley."

His mother sipped her soda, staring across the living room. "I love you, Dylan, and I've tried to make sure you and your brothers had what you needed and always felt loved." She wiped her cheek.

"Mom, why are you crying?"

"I'm so proud of you. You're an amazing young man, but since the day your father died, you've never been able to love."

"That's not true. I love you. My brothers and their families. Hell, I've even learned how to hold a baby and not freak out."

That made his mother chuckle.

"That's not what I mean. Logan loved Mia since high school. He didn't know it, but I think because they always had some contact, his heart never broke, but he also never stopped loving her."

"Not everyone wants to get married, and I'm in that category."

"I'm not talking about marriage. I'm talking about the kind of love that can rip your heart out in a second. Nick and I both know what it's like to lose a spouse. I loved…still love, your father so much that I can't go to his grave without bawling like a baby. He's still the first thing I think of when I wake up and the last person I think of before I go to bed. I dream about him all the time, and I know he's never coming back and I so worried that Nick would do what you have done when he lost Joanne."

Carefully, Dylan sat up, securing the boot back over

his damaged ankle and took his mother's hands. "What are you talking about?"

"I remember it took all of Ramey's might to get you off that hospital bed."

"I don't want to do this. Dad's death affected all of us, and rehashing it like this isn't going to change anything." He swallowed. Hard. Hearing himself say those words made him realize how deep he'd pushed those feelings of pain and suffering. That he still did. That even with writing in the journal and talking through some things, he never really let himself feel anything other than responsibility.

And not the good kind. No, he took on the world, making everything his problem. His fault.

His mother blinked her eyes a few times, glaring through the tears. "You need to let me finish, okay?"

He nodded, rubbing his thumbs over the tops of her hands.

"You were crying so hard and hugging your father so tight. The nurse said you'd been like that for a good ten minutes by the time Ramey and I got there."

"I tried to punch Ramey," Dylan said softly.

"Ramey always knew how to avoid a fist," his mother said with a slight smile. "Minutes later, you stopped crying. Your body stiffened. And it was like the light of hope in your eyes faded into the background. You told us all what Dad said and answered all our questions with not a single emotion. Your tone was flat, and I kept trying to find that light that my little Dylan always had."

"It was a hard day and I was just trying to do what Dad asked." Dylan bit back a sob that bellowed from his gut.

"Over the years, I saw that light every once in a while. The day I dropped you off at West Point, I saw it. The first time you got to work with Ramey in the Army, I saw it. I even saw it the first time you held your nieces and nephews. I saw it yesterday when you told me what the doctor said, and that's more why I got mad because I knew, even though your heart wants to care more about Kinsley, you're never going to love a woman. I thought you were just fumbling around like Logan and Ramey, believing that someday, a woman was going to knock you on your ass. I worried that Nick would never allow himself to love again, but at least I knew he was capable."

Dylan yanked his hands free. "You're saying I'm not capable of loving someone? That I'm cold-hearted?"

His mother nodded. "I have to accept that about you because I want to see that light shine again, and if the only thing that will give that to you is Delta Force, then so be it."

"You're wrong, Mom."

"Am I?" she asked with an arched brow.

"I'll give you that I love what I do. I'll even agree that I don't know how to deal with emotional crap, so I just push it aside. But I most definitely am capable of loving a woman. I just don't want to right now."

His mother wiped her tears. "Do you think Ramey wanted to fall in love when he was happy flying crazy fast and upside down in planes that were probably going to crash half the time? He wasn't prepared for Tequila, but he at least opened his heart. If you walk away from every girl you meet because you don't want to find out if she'll mean at least as much to you as Delta Force, then you will never be capable of loving."

"That's fucking harsh, Mom."

"Don't swear in my house, and I call them like I see them."

"I'm sorry for the language, but I've got a question for you. Why haven't you given another man a chance? Are you going to mourn Dad forever?"

"If you hadn't been beaten so badly, I'd be slapping your face right now, young man." She reached up and tugged at his ear, which was worse than being slapped. "Of course, I'm going to mourn him forever. Just like Nick will always have Joanne in his heart, even though he's with Leandra now and loves her with all his heart and soul. For years, I didn't date because it's not easy raising boys all by yourself. Granted, only two of you were home, but still. And the few times I've dated, which I have, but you wouldn't know because you're only home for a couple of days at a time, I just didn't feel much but a sort of kind affection for them. It's not that I don't want to find another man to share my life with, it's that I haven't found him yet. But damn it, at least I'm open to it. You, on the other hand, won't even give it a try because you're too afraid it's going to hurt. You can endure all sorts of physical pain, but emotional? Nope. You won't go there. Well, guess what? Loving someone always hurts. Now if you'll excuse me, I'm going out for the day." She released his ear. "You're on your own for dinner."

He stood in the middle of the family room while his mother stormed off, slamming the door shut behind her.

His chest tightened. He couldn't let her leave like that.

Limping out of the house and toward the carport, he managed to reach his mom before she got in her car. "Mom, wait," he said, sucking in a deep breath. "Please, don't leave like this."

She tossed her purse across the driver's seat. "I didn't mean to be so brutal."

"It's okay." He pulled her in for a hug. "I don't know how to process all this, but I love you, and I can't stand that I've hurt you or that you worry so much."

"When you're a mother, you always worry. No matter how old your kids get. It's part of the deal." She lifted her chin, glancing up at him. "You've been through hell and back. I just want you happy. That's all I've ever wanted."

"I know. Do you mind if I take off for a couple of days? I thought I'd go camping and really think about what you said. What Kinsley said."

"You're a grown man. You don't need my permission. Just promise me, this isn't you running, but you dealing with what's going on in here." She pressed her hand on the center of his chest.

"I'm not running, I promise. I'll text you throughout the next couple of days."

She patted his cheek. "You're good man, Dylan. A bit broken maybe, but you're a keeper."

He was glad his mother thought so, but he wasn't so sure. He glanced over his shoulder to see Kinsley get into her car. He waved but got no response. He tried to get her to stop, but she drove the other direction and out the other gate.

He owed her an apology, big time.

13

*D*ylan rolled the Jeep to a stop in the street in front of his mother's house right behind his brother Ramey's SUV. Dylan ended up camping until Thursday, a few more days longer than he'd originally planned.

But he needed to be left alone with nothing but his thoughts.

And dreams.

And private tears.

And journals.

He'd written so much it hurt his hand, but when he read the words, it made his heart hurt.

Actually, it crushed what was left of it.

Dylan had no idea what love felt like, but he knew what it looked like, and when he saw Kinsley or even thought about her, it reminded him of his parents and his brothers, and that freaked him right the fuck out.

He noticed Kinsley's car wasn't in the driveway.

It was only five in the evening, so she was probably still at work. He only wished she would have called him back, or at least texted him about his apology.

The front of his mother's house crashed open.

"Uncle Baby Dyl!" Kayla shouted as she grabbed hold of the railing with her chubby, little hands, her mother, Tequila, trying to guide her, but Kayla was a Sarich through and through and no way did she need any help, even if that meant crash-landing on her pretty little face. Her blonde curls bounced with each step she took. Once she hit the sidewalk, she was off and running, hands flapping at her sides, her body zig-zagging like a drunk sailor.

Dylan kneeled down with his arms wide open.

"Be careful, Kayla. Remember your uncle has some pretty bad boo-boos," Tequila said, leaning against the stairs.

"You tell that husband of yours he's going to have some boo-boos if he keeps telling this one to call me Baby Dyl."

Kayla leapt into his arms, smashing against his sore rib, but he didn't care. He held his niece close, smelling her honeysuckle baby shampoo. "But Daddy says you like it when I call you that."

"I'd rather you call me Uncle Dylan," he whispered into her ear, kissing her plump cheek.

She pulled her head back, cupping his face with her hands and smacking her lips against his. "I'm gonna be a big sister!"

"So I've heard. Do me a favor and never call your little brother or sister, baby anything, okay?"

"Okay." Kayla wiggled and kicked her feet. "Mommy said I could ride my Jeep around the block."

"Sounds like a blast! Where is your dad?"

"I'm right here," Ramey said, stepping around the side of the house, pushing a brand-new motorized toy Jeep. "She wants to drive monster trucks this week."

"I'm gonna be the best one ever!" She scrunched up her face as Dylan set her down. "I'm gonna smash up and drive over all the other rucks!"

Dylan laughed.

"You set that sucker to l-o-w?" Tequila asked.

"Oh yeah, especially because she d-r-i-v-e-s like her mother," Ramey said.

"Hey, you crashed more planes in your career than I did." Tequila followed Kayla as she pulled the Jeep onto the street.

"Um, hello. I was in the Army longer and was a test pilot longer, so I think—"

"Is everything a contest with you two?" Dylan slapped his brother on the back.

"Keeps things interesting," Ramey said. "Let's get a beer before everyone else shows up."

"They are all coming here? Damn, this house can't handle eight adults and five kids."

"We're just meeting here and then walking over to Harbor Village. We rented the big pontiki boat, which might be worse with five kids under the age of three, but there will be beer and wine. Lots of beer and wine."

Dylan laughed.

"You look a lot better, bro."

"I'm feeling a lot better." Though quite confused about life, love, career, and everything in between. Dylan was glad to have a few moments alone with Ramey. While he was close to all his brothers, he and Ramey shared a room growing up and since Ramey was only two years older, their years at West Point crossed over by two. Dylan sat in the rocker on the front porch and accepted the beer his brother handed him. He'd been the only one, except their mom, that had known about the woman Ramey had given his heart to and then left him standing at the altar.

Something they almost never talked about.

"How are the nightmares?"

"I'll be dreaming about the men who died on my watch I'm sure for years, but I did get to the heart of why they were shaking my confidence so much."

"Yeah, and what's that?"

Dylan took a swig of his beer before looking his brother square in the eye. "Dad."

Ramey's eyes went wide. "How so?"

"Well, it's more than Dad, but it starts there and how I internalized everything that happened. Like I was supposed to be the strong one. Make sure you all knew Dad's dying words, and sometimes I felt like you, Logan, and Nick resented me for it."

"We did. We also hated that you had to be the one to be with him, alone."

"That's the key word. Alone." Dylan glanced in the

direction of Kinsley's house. Kayla had made her way one driveway down, so it seemed like he was looking at her, not wondering where Kinsley was.

"You were never alone."

"One for all, and all for one," Dylan said with a laugh. "I know that. But I felt alone. Logan off at college then the Army. Nick married, then he joined the military. You went to West Point. It was just me and Mom, and I could hear her cry every night, and I couldn't do anything to make it go away, and Dad had me promise we'd take care of Mom."

"We all have," Ramey said, reaching over, resting his hand on Dylan's shoulder. "And I was a shit brother to you when you came to West Point."

"Yeah, you were." Dylan laughed. "Of course, I was a plebe, so you had to be."

"But I was also a tad jealous of you."

Dylan cocked his head. "How so?"

"Jesus, you have to ask? You got a perfect score on everything. Smartest kid in that entire place. I made it on being a wiseass, and some people took to that."

"You had no fear, that helped."

Ramey laughed, nodding, but then his face turned serious. "I know you, and something is on your mind, what is it?"

"I thought my dreams were all about this last mission. Ramey, it was bad. I shouldn't tell you this, but I had men dying in my arms, begging me to give their loved ones messages."

"Fuck me," Ramey mumbled. "Just like Dad."

"It certainly brought all that up again."

"You never let it out, Dylan. Once I pulled you off Dad, you became a walking zombie. We all waited for you to fall apart. Logan thought it would be at Dad's funeral. Nick and I figured you'd do it in private. You were always so reserved, even before Dad died. But have you ever really let yourself mourn Dad?"

Dylan didn't mean to laugh, but he found the comment funny considering his conversation with his mother. "I haven't. Not really. I think somewhere in my mind and heart, I thought if I fell apart again, then I'd somehow lose him or something. I've had a lot of weird dreams about Dad over the years, but in the Army—in Delta Force—it's allowed me to stay numb and yet alive at the same time."

"Oh, bro, I know that feeling. As fucked up as this will sound, the first test plane that I had to crash-land made me feel like that last day we all went fishing."

"Exactly," Dylan whispered.

"But trust me when I tell you, that's not the same feeling at all. I know we all are adrenaline junkies. Dad was too. But what I felt when I pushed the limits wasn't really what we all felt that day. Loving Tequila and being a dad, that's brought me back to that day, and every day of my childhood. That's the kind of rush a man can live on forever."

"Mom doesn't think I'm capable of loving anyone," Dylan blurted out.

"She actually said that?" Ramey held his beer up

with his mouth gaping open. "I thought she was going to try to push the sexy doctor next door on you."

"She didn't have to push too hard for something to happen."

"Damn, you know we work with her father." Ramey leaned back in his chair, nursing his beer, staring out over the water.

"So I've heard." Dylan heard Kayla's laughter echo off the water as she raced her little Jeep down the street. Sweetest noise ever. "I really fucked that up."

"What do you mean?"

"Last time I saw Kinsley, she told me to get the fuck out of her house and not to come back."

"Ouch. What did you do?"

"I pulled a Ramey," Dylan said, raising his longneck.

"You stupid little shit. I was so angry at women for so long, I really knew how to hurt them. Why the hell would you do that? You've never been dumped by someone you really cared about...holy shit. You care about her, don't you?"

"And here, you thought I was the smart one," Dylan said with a smirk.

"I'll be hog-tied. Baby Dyl is in love."

"Goddamnit, Ramey. Why the fuck do you have to call me that? You know I hate it."

"Don't change the subject," Ramey said. "And geez, you have to admit where Mom and Dad got your name is funny. I mean, I was two when you were born, and Mom was always eating pickles so when I came to see you, I called you baby Dyl, and they named you Dylan. Not my fault."

"Yeah, it is and now you have your daughter calling me that."

Ramey laughed. "We can go down the baby Dyl rabbit hole to avoid the fact that you have your first taste of what it's like to be in love all you want. But you're going to have to face it and make a decision."

"Kinsley may have already made it for me," Dylan said as three cars pulled into the driveway. "Looks like the gang is all here."

14

*K*insley watched from her family room window as most of Dylan's family piled into their vehicles. It had been nice to hear the sound of laughing children as they ran about in the front yard as the sun set over the Intracoastal Waterway. Even nicer to see Dylan with a big smile on his face.

She'd kept her lights off, both outside and inside, but she was sure, if he looked, he'd see the light from her television through the window. Setting her glass of wine on the table, she reached for her phone and listened to his heartfelt apology once more. She was about to open the text thread to read those when a new message lit up her screen.

*D*ylan: *Please let me apologize in person. I'm standing on your front porch. I'll be here all night, waiting if I have to.*

*W*ell, fuck. She couldn't hide from him forever.

*K*insley: *Door's unlocked. Come on in.*

*S*econds later, he stood in front of her. "May I?" He waved to the sofa.

She moved over. "I accept your apology."

"What I said was mean and served only to hurt you."

"I know," she said, taking a sip of her wine. "I tried to manipulate you and that was wrong." Being next to him made her heart melt and drip all over her soul.

"I didn't mean to imply that you get off on—"

She covered his mouth with her hand. "I know you didn't. You were making a point that we both don't do relationships. What bothered me is that you lied to me and then you tossed your dream in my face to embarrass me."

He let out a long breath. "I did it to hurt you, and I was still lying. I didn't have that dream about my father, at least not that night."

She cocked her head. "Why did you lie?"

"Because the dream was about you, and it scared me in ways I can't even describe because I've never felt like this before."

"Oh. I think I need another drink."

"Me too. Do you have an open bottle?" He stood, heading toward the counter she used for a bar off the family room.

"Just cracked it open."

Knowing her hands trembled, she quickly snagged her glass, holding it against her chest, hoping to squelch the nervous twitch.

He returned, filled their glasses, and sat down, shifting his body, facing her.

She, on the other hand, kept her eyes on the television. "I don't want you to feel like you have to tell me about the dream you had. Like I said before, dreams aren't always what we think they are."

"I know that. But I also know I've never let myself grieve for my father. I've been running from it ever since Ramey made me let him go after he died. I use my career as a way of paying omiyage to him, I guess. My dad was my hero and when he died, and my brothers scattered to different places, I felt alone, even though I wasn't. Delta Force gave me a different kind of home. One where all I had to care about was the men, and the mission."

"Just like your dad and brothers. You have a very special family," she said, turning her head, catching his gaze, giving him the respect he so rightfully deserved. "And your brothers all have families of their own now."

"And my men are dead."

"That's not your fault," she said, curling her fingers

around his strong biceps. "You have to stop beating yourself up over this."

He tilted her chin up with his thumb and forefinger. "That's not what this is about. I'd been having weird dreams about my dad since before this last mission. While I know my brothers always have my back, I felt like I couldn't ask them. They have wives and children. That sense of loneliness crept in, only I didn't know I was lonely until I met you and even then, I didn't get it until my mother told me I was incapable of loving a woman."

Kinsley bit down on her lower lip, trying not to burst into laughter.

"It's not funny."

"I just can't picture your mother saying something like that. She thinks everyone should be in love. She's almost as bad as my mother, only Catherine at least gets lust is not love."

"And that's where I'm confused." He took a long, slow sip of his wine.

She opted to say nothing because she didn't want to jump to any conclusion that might be wrong, and she wasn't even sure how she felt, so best to let him finish his thought.

"I've never been in love. I had a few girlfriends in high school, and I dated one girl for like a year when I was at West Point, but she told me I had the emotional capacity of a two-year-old which now makes me laugh because my nieces and nephews are the most incredibly emotional beings ever."

"Children wear their feelings on their sleeves. But I get what she meant."

"I didn't, but I do now. I honestly don't know what I want anymore. In my dream that morning, you were running away from me, but I wasn't chasing you. While I think you're hot, what I feel is more than lust, but I don't know if I can even go there, and I know you don't want to."

"Dylan," she said, resting her hand on his thigh. "I don't know either. You have a lot of things you need to work through right now, and I want to be there for you. I really do. But I have my own issues with love and trust and the fact you had the ability to hurt me so badly, that scared me."

"So, what are we to do about all this? Because I really do want to see where this might lead." He dropped his head back on the sofa and closed his eyes. "Did I just say that out loud?"

"Yep, you did." She chugged her wine, then set the glass on the table. "You're leaving in a couple of days and long distance, with deployments, don't make for an easy go of it."

"Nope. They don't," he blinked open his eyes. "And that brings us right back to where we started." He stood, resting his hands on her hips. "I don't think I can give up Delta Force."

"And I wouldn't ask you to because I don't know if I'm capable of even giving myself to anyone completely. I've never been in love either, and I don't know if I can open myself up that much."

"I'm an asshole for wanting to spend the night anyway."

"No. You're not. But I'm not going to let you. I can't do a long-distance thing with someone in the military no matter how much I care about them."

He kissed the tip of her nose. "You're still going to come tomorrow and sit with my family, right?"

She nodded.

He let out a long sigh and turned. "Good night, Kinsley."

"Sleep well, Dylan."

She watched him leave, holding back the tears. Oh, she knew she could open her heart to love because she loved him.

But he wasn't ready to give up Delta Force, he even said so, and who the hell was she to ask him to anyway? She picked up her phone and did the unthinkable. "Hey, Siri, call Mom."

It took only one ring.

"Hey, Kinsley. It's late. Is everything okay?"

"No, Mom. It's not." She plopped back down on the sofa, shoving the wine away. That's the last thing she needed. "I just saw Dylan."

"Oh dear, what happened?"

When she'd kicked Dylan out of her house that morning, she ran right to her mother, who was having breakfast alone after surprisingly not spending the night with that man. Turns out, her mother was still madly in love with husband number six and wanted him back in the worst way. She'd never seen her mother like that. They spent the day together, walking the beach, talking, and it was like she'd finally understood what her mother was all about.

Still a bit crazy, but their relationship had moved forward and during that day, she confided in her mother all that had happened with Dylan.

Well, most of it. She left out his nightmares. That wasn't hers to tell.

"He wanted to apologize in person and I accepted it, but we still ended up with him going back to Delta Force, and I can't do that, Mom. I just can't. It was so hard when Daddy was on active duty and sometimes I wonder if he gave that up too soon to help raise me."

"I know I wasn't the best mother, and I could have done better but let me tell you something about your dad. He'd been talking about leaving the military for two years before he actually did it. Meeting the men who started Aegis made him realize he could do good somewhere else and be a better parent to you."

Kinsley glanced out the window. Dylan had disappeared. "Mom, did you ever ask Dad to leave the military?"

"No. I never did, and he offered a few times."

"Dylan didn't offer," she said quietly. "Maybe I shouldn't go tomorrow."

"Oh yes, you should. You go and stand with his family. You honor what he has done for this country, and you let him know that you care very much for him. You tell him how you feel and then you let things fall as they may. But, dear, by not telling him you love him, you're not really giving him the full picture and how can he honestly know what he wants when he's just as afraid as you are?"

"I hate it when you make sense."

"Only happens once in a blue moon. I've got to pack."

"Pack? Where are you going?"

"Home. We're going to give it another go."

"That's wonderful, Mom. I love you." She tapped the red button and set the phone on the table.

Would she be able to tell Dylan how she really felt?

What was the worst thing that could happen? He'd leave.

Well, he was doing that anyway.

---

*I*t seemed like it took forever for him to make it back to his mother's house. When he stepped inside, Ramey sat in the recliner with a passed out eighteen-month-old on his lap. "Tequila," Ramey whispered. "Mind taking this little one to bed?"

"Not at all," Tequila said as she rose from the sofa, scooping up her daughter. "Are you okay?" she asked, staring at Dylan.

"I will be."

She nodded before disappearing into what used to be Nick and Logan's room.

"I was kind of hoping we wouldn't see you tonight," Ramey said.

Dylan leaned against the wall between the family room and the kitchen. "I was kind of hoping that myself, but this time I think it's more her, than me. Her mother's been married like six times and is divorcing this latest one."

"I've heard about her mom, from Kinsley's dad."

"Well, Kinsley basically flat-out told me besides not wanting a long-distance thing with a military man, she doesn't think she could ever open herself up to love."

Ramey pushed the level on the chair and stood, facing his brother with his hands on his hips. "Have you considered she might be saying the latter because the former is what scares her, not love."

"What?"

"You're homeless and having quarters in Ft. Bragg is not a home. Living on the edge, you can't do that forever, but you do have other options. I might not fly upside down as often as I used to, but I do get to occasionally jump out of a perfectly good airplane and some of the jobs we go on, as you know since you've helped out with a few, have their dangerous, adrenaline-packed moments that we all need every once in a while. We do have to travel, and that's often hard on the wives and the kids, but it's not over two hundred days a year."

"You're suggesting I take a job with Aegis."

"I think you should consider it, and I think you need to tell Kinsley how you really feel."

Dylan blinked. His brain was having a hard time wrapping around that conversation and how it might go. He had six months left before he signed his re-enlistment papers. And what if it didn't work out with Kinsley? What then? At least if he tried it while in Delta... "Thanks, but I'm staying in Delta Force."

15

"War is something many of us will never have to experience. We will see it on the news. Read about it in the papers. Hear stories from veterans. Many of these stories will tug at our hearts and rip our souls."

Dylan listened to General Maxwell while seated with his brothers on a small stage. His mother, his brothers' wives, their children, Kinsley, and a few other close family friends sat in front of the stage while a large crowd had gathered behind them. He could see old friends from high school. Teachers. Even his old baseball coach. He wanted to believe he deserved the honor, but part of him still felt like he'd failed his men.

Failed the mission.

Failed his father and brothers.

He pushed those negative thoughts out of his mind and focused on Kinsley. She made him feel different about things. If this had happened to anyone else, and they were getting these medals, he'd know they were deserving.

"We can empathize and sympathize with the families who have lost loves ones to war. We honor those who have died while serving this country in the name of liberty and freedom. But what about those men and women who survive? What about those men and women who fight next to those we don't get to bring home? What about those men and women who show courage and bravery in the face of catastrophe? We don't always hear about them. We hear about the successful missions and the courageous men who lost their lives. But we don't always hear about the one who made it back when his entire team had been captured behind enemy lines."

Dylan had heard that earlier this morning, the president had given a statement about what had really happened. Well, not all of it, but enough that it might help give those families who lost someone closure.

"For the safety of our troops, we can't always give details and perhaps, those details are often too devastating to fathom. Even I, a general in the Army, cannot truly understand or even imagine what Major Dylan James Sarich endured while being tortured in captivity." General Maxwell glanced over his shoulder. With us today are former Sergeant Major Logan Michael Sarich and former Command Sergeant Major Nicolaus Emmerson Sarich, both of whom served under my command. I gave the commencement speech at West Point, my alma mater, when former Captain Ramey

Jordan Sarich graduated. I am here to tell you these are some of the finest men around and I ask Logan, Nick, and Ramey, as I have to come to know them, to please join me in honoring their brother."

No one ever told Dylan that when you opened the emotional flood gates, there might be no shutting them. He quickly ran a finger across his cheeks.

These weren't sad tears, though. He was proud of his brothers, and they deserved to here after what they had done while serving their country. A little chuckle echoed in the back of his mind. Kinsley had been right about everything. He watched his brothers take their places next to the general with a sense of pride and awe.

A wave of never having to be alone coursed through his body like a runaway freight train.

General Maxwell handed a small box to Ramey and nodded to Dylan. He stood at attention.

"At ease," the general said.

Dylan relaxed, but his heart raced as he stared at Kinsley, who held baby Emmerson in her arms.

"Major Sarich, it is with great honor and pride that I have been chosen to award you with the Medal of Honor, for your heroism in combat. It is not just this one mission that makes you deserving of this medal. It is all your years of service, risking your life day in and day out so that the citizens of the United States can sleep easy at night."

Dylan stepped in front of General Maxwell while his brother opened the box and handed it to him.

The general handed another box to Ramey. "Today we not only honor your heroism for all your years of service but recognize how fragile life is. I cannot say that is with great pleasure that I award you the Purple Heart, for the life-threatening wounds you have suffered during combat, for I am humbled by your bravery. Your strength. Your courage. You are more than a good soldier. You are a good man, and it has been an honor to serve with you. I want to personally thank you for your service and welcome you home."

Ramey opened the box and handed it to Dylan.

"Thank you, sir," Dylan said softly, his eyes filling with tears. The boxes felt overwhelmingly heavy in his hands. He stood next to his brothers, feeling like his knees might give out at any second.

"I want to thank everyone for coming," General Maxwell said. "Today we celebrate our independence and because of men like Major Dylan James Sarich, we will continue to enjoy our freedom."

The crowd erupted in cheers, and all Dylan wanted to do was to get the hell out of Dodge, but he knew that would be impossible. There were interviews lined up with a few local and national news crews. Nothing special. Nothing too fancy, but it would take a few hours.

After that, over to Kinsley's to tell her he loved her. He wished he'd been able to do it this morning, but everyone kept getting in the way.

"I'm really kind of glad that's over," Dylan said as he followed his brothers off the stage.

"I love that I outranked Logan," Nick said.

"Hey, I outrank all of you idiots," Dylan said.

"Who would have thunk that Baby Dyl would surpass my rank," Ramey said.

"Asshole," Dylan muttered with a chuckle just as his mother came running up.

"I love that you were honored but if you ever go get yourself captured and tortured again, I will more than do this." She reached up and yanked at his ear.

"Mom. Stop. It's so embarrassing, especially in front of General Maxwell."

"That's how you keep these Sarich boys in line," Leandra said as she took a crying Emmerson out of Kinsley's hands.

"My mother used to do the same thing. Drove me nuts." General Maxwell laughed. "Mrs. Sarich, you have an amazing family."

"I will take all the credit, thank you very much," she said with a smile.

Dylan laughed as he took a water from the table under the tent just off to the right of the stage, away from the crowd.

"It was a real honor to see all of you boys again. Amazing that I worked with each of you at different times."

"Be glad you didn't work with us all at once," Logan said. "You think I was a smartass, the four of us on one mission using the same comms link, you'd have all our heads on that famous platter of yours."

"I think the four of you all on the same team would be interestingly amazing."

"As long as Ramey isn't at the helm of a plane," Tequila said. "I'm so much better, so that should be my job."

"You must be Ramey's wife. I've heard some stories about you from some of my buddies over at the Air Force Academy. You're quite the little firecracker."

"No, I'm the cracker," Kayla yelled as she danced around her mother's legs, her cousins chasing her.

"General, these are my other two daughters-in-law, Mia and Leandra," his mother said.

"Oh, Mia, the computer hacker, right?" General Maxwell asked. "And Leandra, I met your father a long time ago. Good man."

"You sure do get around," Dylan said with a smile. "See, I can be a smartass like my brother."

"I used to tease him that he was too serious for his own good," the general said. "And that joke needs work."

"Yes, sir," Dylan said as he hobbled two steps to his right, tugging at Kinsley's arm, pulling her closer, even though she gave him a weird look and tried moving in the other direction. "General Maxwell, this is my friend, Kinsley. Her dad works with my brothers at Aegis."

The general arched a brow. "It's nice to meet you, Dylan's friend, though you look awfully familiar."

"Actually, I met you when I was three and a few

times after that. My dad is retired Green Beret, Wesley Maron."

"Holy shit. I really do get around. You're little Kinsley Maron, the girl that analyzed everything right down to giving away a man's tell in a game of poker. How the hell is your dad? I haven't seen him since he left my command. I'm still holding a grudge and want a rematch."

Kinsley smiled. "He still has that hundred-dollar bill hanging on his home office wall and still tells everyone how I kicked your ass in poker at the age of twelve."

"Don't let this girl near a poker table unless you want to lose your money, other than that, you picked a fine girl to have on your arm," General Maxwell said, slapping Dylan on the back. "I best let you go. Those reporters over there are looking hungry."

"Thanks for doing this. It meant a lot to me coming from you." Dylan snapped to attention and saluted the general.

He saluted back. "I'll see you around, kid."

"We'll see you at home," his mother said, trying to help wrestle all the grandkids. "Kinsley, you can ride with me."

"Give us one second, okay, Mom?"

"I'll be at the car."

"I should go," Kinsley said, stepping back. "Stop by in the morning before you head for Bragg."

"Wait. I need to talk to you. Can I stop by tonight?"

"You should be with your family."

"Everyone but Ramey is staying at the Vanderlins'

and with kids, they will all be leaving by dark. Please. I really need to see you."

"All right. But not if it's going to be after ten."

"Deal." Without giving it much thought, he bent over and brushed his lips tenderly against hers, circling his arms around her waist.

Her fists landed on his shoulders, and he knew he should have backed away, but instead, he deepened the kiss, tentatively at first, but when her tongue engaged with his, he found himself on a mission to show her just how much he cared.

"Dylan," she whispered, pushing away. "You can't come over if you're going to do that."

He swallowed. Hard.

He planned on doing that and a whole lot more.

"I just want to talk to you."

She nodded and walked away.

When he turned, three cameras were pointed in his face and one photographer was still snapping pictures.

"Is that your girlfriend?" one reporter asked with a mic shoved in his face.

Shit. Kinsley wasn't going to like seeing that kiss plastered all over the news.

"Holy shit," Kinsley mumbled as her face turned beet red sitting on the sofa in Catherine's house. Leandra was on one side, Mia on the other, while Tequila and Catherine sat on the floor with the kids.

"Mommy, Uncle Baby Dyl is kissing Kinsley," Kayla said.

"That's gross," Abigail, Logan's daughter, yelled.

"No, it's not," Tyler, Nick's two-year-old, said, climbing on the recliner to be on his father's lap. "Everyone kisses everyone." He grabbed his dad's face and gave him a big kiss on the cheek. "See."

"That's a different kind of kissing," Nick said.

"Really. You have to go there with him?" Leandra shook her head. "He's girl crazy as it is."

"He's a Sarich, what do you expect," Catherine said. "Turn up the volume."

The image switched to the local anchor. "We'll be right back with more coverage from today's parade, an interview with Major Dylan James Sarich where we all hope he'll tell us who that young woman was."

"Oh, this should be good," Logan said, plopping down on the floor in front of Mia, holding Michael in his lap with a bottle.

The news cut out to commercial.

Kinsley sank deeper into the sofa. She wanted to run and hide. She shouldn't have ever let his family talk her into coming over for dinner and drinks.

"Dylan should have been home by now," Ramey said from his perch on a folding chair. "We are taping this, aren't we?"

"God, I hope not." Dylan walked through the front door.

"We saw you kissing Kinsley!" Tyler said, puckering his lips, making smacking noises.

"I kind of hope she's not watching this." Dylan yanked one of the kitchen chairs to pull it closer to the family room. "I need to talk with her first, but she wasn't home."

"Um, Baby Dyl," Ramey said, pointing his finger to the couch. "She's right there."

"You come sit over here," Leandra said, standing with Emmerson in her arms. I'll go sit in front of Nick."

"No. I think I'm fine right here," Dylan said.

Kinsley blinked her eyes a few times, taking in long breaths, examining potential escape routes, but she knew this family would stop her, and that might make this situation worse.

"I insist." Leandra kicked his good leg. "Go sit on the sofa and put your bad leg up on the coffee table."

"Yeah, why don't you go do that, Baby Dyl," Ramey said with a huge smile.

"You're lucky children are here," Dylan said behind a clenched jaw as he took a seat next to Kinsley.

"Hey," he said. "How are things going?"

"I don't know, you tell me?" Kinsley asked with wide eyes.

"We really don't want to watch this in front of my family," he whispered.

"Do I want to watch this at all?"

"Probably not. I was hoping to talk to you first, but all the interviews lasted longer than expected and just so you know, they all got that kiss, and they all asked me about it."

"My father is going to see that."

"He's texted me twice," Logan said. "You might want to check your phone."

"It's in my purse," Kinsley said. Her voice rattled like a scared rabbit. She wasn't worried about what her father would say, but she was sure as hell worried about what Dylan said.

Or didn't say.

"I can get it for you." Catherine snagged it off the counter. "Can I—"

"The news is back on," Ramey said. "I can't wait to hear this."

"I'm here with Major Dylan Sarich who was just awarded the Medal of Honor and the Purple Heart. He was here with his entire family and one very special lady." The camera panned from the reporter to Dylan, who looked like someone tied a noose around his neck. *"Today was about honoring your service, your heroism, and all the sacrifices you have made for this country. It was a touching speech the general gave and amazing he knew and served with you and all your brothers."*

"It was a privilege for me to have him and my brothers here today. I accept the medals in honor of all my fallen brothers. It's them who really deserve to be remembered for their great acts of heroism."

"I can't imagine how hard it must have been for your family when they got word you went missing."

"Actually, due to the nature of the mission, they didn't

know until after I had been extracted and taken to Germany."

"That sounded horrible," his mother muttered.

"It's true," Ramey said. "And it was best we didn't know until after. It would have been weeks of hell not knowing."

"I agree," Logan said.

"Shhhhh," Nick said.

"Still, it must have been hard on your family, especially the young woman you were kissing just moments ago."

Dylan cleared his throat. "War is never easy."

"You dodge that question well," Nick said with a sarcastic laugh.

"Not even close," Dylan mumbled.

"I feel sick to my stomach." Kinsley leaned closer to Dylan and whispered, which was a mistake because everyone was staring at her and not the television.

"We understand you are with the Elite group, Delta Force. Since what has happened, will you be able to return to active duty? Do you plan on returning? And what does your girlfriend have to say about that? And while I'm on that subject, what is her name?"

"I don't know if I will be able to return to the same role I had. I'm currently on medical leave, and I will possibly need another surgery on my foot. I will need to pass a very diffi-cult physical once I'm healed, and trust me when I say, it was the hardest test I've ever had to take and I don't look forward to taking it again, which is in part, why I am considering not returning to Delta Force."

"Holy shit," Logan said.

His mother grabbed his ear. "Children in the room."

"I think holy something else is in order," Nick said.

"Why would you say that?" Kinsley snapped her gaze toward Dylan.

"At this point, we might as well listen to the rest of the interview." He pressed his finger on her lips then pointed to the television.

Her heart hammered against her ribs like a woodpecker.

"Will you stay in the Army?" the reporter asked.

"I'm not sure. After the ceremony, my brothers and I had a chance to talk with General Maxwell and we joked about what it would be like for all four of us to be on the same team. I mean, we've all worked special jobs together, but not in anything permanent. But all three of them work for the Aegis Network, which is a group of men and women, mostly ex-military, police, and those types of professions who use their specialized skills in different ways that help protect and serve the community. It also gives them the chance to spend more time with their wives and children."

"Does this mean you're not only planning on joining the Aegis Network, but settling down as well?"

"Oh my God," Kinsley said, covering her mouth as she stood. "I think I need to—"

"I will be looking into resigning from the Army and working with my brothers at the Aegis Network. The more I think about that, the more I really want to do it. You don't find men better than those three, and our father always told us to have each other's back. What better way to honor our dad than to actually work together. As far as the settling

down part goes, well, yeah. But I kind of haven't really talked to Kinsley about that, so when I get home tonight, I'm going to have some explaining to do."

"I would say so. Well, we wish you the best of luck and thank you once again for your service."

Someone clicked off the television. The room went deadpan silent.

"Excuse me." Kinsley sidestepped those sitting on the floor. Hell, she didn't even know at this point who was where. All she knew was every time she tried to suck in a breath, she nearly choked. "I need some air." She gripped the door as a wave of nausea rose from deep in the pit of her stomach, smacking the back of her mouth like a pebble skipping across the water.

"Maybe you should sit down," a female voice said. Could have been Catherine, but Kinsley wasn't so sure.

"Air. Just air," Kinsley said as she managed to step outside, but the thick, humid Florida air only clung to the insides of her lungs, making her feel like someone had a hold on her neck, not allowing her to breath.

"Kinsley, sit down." Dylan came up behind her and helped her to one of the chairs on his mother's porch. "I didn't mean for you to hear all that on the news, in front of my family."

She took the glass of water he offered. "I could really use something stronger after that news show."

"In that case, let's go to your place, because I'm not going back in there."

"You can't go back in there? How do you think I feel?"

"I really don't know, but can I tell you how I feel?"

She blinked a few times, trying to focus on his face. "Did you mean what you said to that reporter?"

"Yes."

"Wow."

"I know," he whispered. "I know you said you don't do relationships, and maybe I'm just being a fool, but God, I want so badly to be with you. This isn't lust, or even heavy like. I used to close my eyes and all I could see was the next mission. The next time I got to put my life on the line. Now I close them, and all I see is you. I was crazy to tell you I couldn't give up Delta Force. Of course, I can give that up to have a chance at something with you. I lov—"

She covered his mouth. "Nope. You don't get to blurt that out just yet."

"Why not?"

"Because I haven't processed any of this. I mean, everyone heard you state you were leaving something you love because of me. I can't be responsible for that. I need to—"

"Did you not hear me?" He bolted from his seat and groaned, bending over and clutching his boot. "This isn't just about you and me. It's about me and my brothers. Standing with them today, I knew I wanted to work with them. So, even if you don't love me, though I think you do but you're more stubborn than I am, I'm still leaving the Army and going to work for Aegis. So, really, don't sweat it. I didn't do it for you." He stood up tall. "Go ahead. Process whatever you need to. I still have to go to Ft. Bragg in a week or so. I still have six months left on my contract, but it won't be on deployment. They will put me behind a desk but guess what. I won't be miserable because I know what I want and that includes you. I love you, whether you want to hear it or not." He turned, shaking his head, and disappeared into the house.

"Fuck," she muttered, chasing him inside. "Oh no, you don't, Dylan James Sarich." His full name rolled off her tongue like she'd been saying it for years.

"Don't what?" He stopped in the kitchen, turned, and glared at her.

"Walk away from me when we're not done talking."

"You said you need time to process. I'm giving that to you."

"You never let me finish my statement before you went off ranting," she said, sucking in a deep breath, painfully aware that his entire family was staring at them.

"By all means, finish." He waved his hand in the air in a flippant gesture.

"When you cut me off, I was about to say that I needed to know that you weren't leaving the Army for me, but for yourself. Yesterday you said you couldn't give up Delta Force. And I understood why, and I couldn't ask you to change that for me."

"And you told me you couldn't live that life and didn't think you could love anyone."

"I can't live that life and you wouldn't ask me to, now would you?"

He shook his head. "But you still said you couldn't—"

"I lied."

"Why?" he asked.

"Because I'm scared of how much I love you, and now I'm going to have to move my practice to Orlando, which is fine. My father is there, and I love Orlando as much as I love it here. But don't think I'm coming to Ft. Bragg with you. I hate that base so for six months we'll have to long-distance it."

"Everyone hates it there," Logan said, laughing.

"I hope someone recorded that," Ramey said. "Better than the news show."

"Don't just stand there, you idiot. Kiss the girl," his mother said, tugging at his ear.

"I think I'd like to do that in private." He took Kinsley's hand and led her outside to the porch where he took her into his arms. "I love you," he whispered.

It felt right to be with him. She smiled. "I love you, too."

EPILOGUE

*D*ylan took the corner into his brother's neighborhood a little too fast, but it had been five days since he'd last seen Kinsley, and five days was five days too many. Didn't matter that they talked on the phone every night. Didn't matter as of yesterday, he'd been discharged from the Army.

And it didn't matter that he knew he'd have the rest of his life to wake up to her pretty face and loving arms.

He slammed the car into park. Ramey's house was only a block from Logan's, and Nick's butted up two houses behind Logan's. Hopefully, Kinsley had found a house for them to buy close by. His heart fluttered like a bunch of bees hanging around honey. Next weekend, they would drive to Jupiter and have a nice little beach wedding with just him, his brothers and their families, his mom, her dad, and her mom and step-father, and of course, General Maxwell.

Even better, in two months, his mom would be moving to Orlando. He and his brothers helped her buy a modest home only a couple miles away. She didn't want to live in the same neighborhood, not because she didn't want to be near them, but the houses were all too big for her, and he could understand that. Hell, they were too big for him and Kinsley, but hopefully, soon, very soon, they'd be adding to the family brood.

Five grandchildren in about four years, with one due in a month, and Logan and Mia decided that two kids just weren't enough, so they were now expecting a new arrival in about five months.

His mother was beside herself.

Now all they had to do was get her married.

Ha! And they had the perfect plan. It was so obvious she and Kinsley's dad were smitten with each other. Now they just had to push them along.

But first things first.

He pounded on Ramey's front door.

A very pregnant Tequila answered the door.

"You look like a house."

"And you look like a dill pickle." She gave him a hug and a kiss. "Everyone is out back."

"Everyone?"

She nodded. "I will warn you. Abigail has learned a new word."

"Oh yeah, what's that?"

"Sex. She overheard her father ask her mother if she wanted to sneak away and have sex in the bathroom to which Mia replied with that's how baby number three happened. So, Abigail is all about finding out exactly what sex is and why it makes babies."

"She just turned four. How is that possible?"

Tequila laughed, patting her belly. "She asked her Uncle Ramey if we made this one in the bathroom too."

"Good Lord. She's going to end up joining the mile-high club."

"Oh, it gets better." Tequila looped her hand in the crook of his arm. "My daughter heard her father say fuck, and it's now her favorite word. Even got Tyler to say it."

"Remind me when I have kids to keep mine away from yours."

Tequila paused. "I still feel like I need to stick a Q-tip in my ear every time you say something like that."

He pulled open the sliding glass doors and prepared himself for the ambush of toddlers.

"Uncle Dylan!" they all yelled, making a beeline for him.

He got down on one knee, so he could hug them all. Well, all but Emmerson, who had started to crawl and pull himself up, but that was about it. Now Michael, who was fifteen months old, nearly barreled over Tyler, who was two and a half.

His ankle still ached, and he rolled it funny as he hugged the kids, giving each of them a big kiss. When he stood, he ended up limping a tad as he made his way to where the adults all sat around a table, sipping beer and wine.

Kinsley stood and did her best not to tackle him when she wrapped her arms around his neck. "This isn't going to be a G-rated kiss."

"Hey, I hear these kids are talking about sex and swearing, I think a little tongue action won't be a problem," he whispered in her ear, before he made true on that statement. "God, I missed you."

"It's only been a week."

"Longest week of my life," he said.

"We've been apart longer," she teased.

"Baby Dyl," Ramey said, slapping him on the back. "Good to have you back."

He'd given up on being upset over his nickname. When he thought about it, it was kind of funny and in a weird way, sweet that his brother had sort of named him. "Looks like you're stuck with me for a while unless my future wife has found us a place to live." He'd originally planned on staying at Nick's, but Tequila wanted the help when the baby was born.

"Oh, we don't mind having you around to help, but I think she did find the perfect place."

"Yeah?" He sat down between Logan and his wife. "Where?"

"The house next to mine just went up for sale," Nick said, handing him a glass of wine. "Though, I don't know how I feel about you being that close to me. I remember when Logan went to college and Mom threatened to move you in with me because you and Ramey constantly fought."

"We didn't fight. We just liked beating the crap out

of each other," Dylan said. "I like the look of the house, but what does the inside look like?"

"Oh, it's amazing," Mia said. "Four bedrooms upstairs and it's got a bedroom and full bath in the basement. Great for when Kinsley's mom comes to visit."

"It's also got two laundry rooms," his mother said as she stepped from the garage carrying a tray of food.

"Where'd you come from?" He stood, limping over to help his mother, aware that everyone stopped and noticed. Even if he hadn't fallen in love with Kinsley, his days in Delta Force would have been over. He had two surgeries and would have to have another one and his leg would never be the same. He could have stayed in the Army, but it wouldn't have been in the field. At least with Aegis, he'd be able to test his limits, be gainfully employed, and spend time with all the people that mattered the most.

"I had left this at Logan's, which is where I'm staying since Mia has horrible morning sickness."

"That sucks," he said, taking the tray as he kissed his mother.

"You know what really sucks," Nick said. "A kid that wakes at three in the morning ready to party. I swear, if we ever get Emmerson to sleep through the night, it will be nothing short of a miracle."

"You didn't sleep through the night until you were two, so it's payback," his mother said.

"Best part is I have Emmerson trained to want his daddy," Leandra said proudly.

Dylan set the tray on the table and sat back down, looping his arm over Kinsley. In a weird way, getting tortured had been a blessing because it brought him to Kinsley.

It brought him home to his family.

And it made him whole again.

"So, can we afford this house?" he asked, leaning in and stealing another kiss.

"We won't have a lot of extra cash, and there is one other slight problem, though it's not a problem, just something we'll have to figure out."

"I don't like the sound of that." Dylan said.

"Neither do I," his mother added. "That house is well in your price range, and you've been building your practice here pretty well. Dylan starts his new job in three weeks. What could be wrong?"

"It's not wrong, just a wrench in our well-laid plans," Kinsley said with a big smile.

"What kind of wrench?" Dylan asked.

"Since our relationship was aired on the national news and has never really been private when it comes to this family, it seems only fitting to tell you in front of everyone, I'm pregnant."

"You're what-gnant?" He literally stuck his finger in his ear and wiggled it. "How did that happen?"

"You had sex in the bathroom," Abigail said matter-of-factly as she climbed on one of the chairs to get some cheese and crackers. "It's how all babies are made. Didn't you know that?"

Everyone at the table bit their lip, trying not to laugh too hard.

Everyone except Dylan. He was still trying to wrap his brain around the word 'pregnant.'

"You're having a baby?" he asked.

"We're having a baby," Kinsley said. "It might be physically coming from my body, but this will be a we program."

"Holy shit," he mumbled. "I'm not ready for this."

"You've got about seven and a half months to get ready," his mother said. "I'm so happy for the both of you."

"A baby," Dylan whispered. He cupped Kinsley's chin. "I love you. I really do and what a nice way to return home."

"You are my home," she said before kissing him.

His father would be so proud.

I want to thank you for taking the time to sit down and read THE RETURN HOME. I hope you enjoyed Dylan and Kinsley's story as much as I did. Please feel free to leave an HONEST review on Amazon and/or Goodreads.

Be on the lookout for Catherine's story, The Matriarch. The Sarich brothers will have fun helping their mother find love again.

Sign up for my Newsletter
(https://dl.bookfunnel.com/rg8mx9lchy).

Join my private Facebook group (https://www.facebook.com/
groups/191706547909047/) where she posts exclusive
excerpts and discuss all things murder and love!

ABOUT THE AUTHOR

Welcome to my World! I'm a USA Today Bestseller of Romantic Suspense, Contemporary Romance, and Paranormal Romance.

I first started writing while carting my kids to one hockey rink after the other, averaging 170 games per year between 3 kids in 2 countries and 5 states. My first book, IN TWO WEEKS was originally published in 2007. In 2010 I helped form a publishing company (Cool Gus Publishing) with NY Times Bestselling Author Bob Mayer where I ran the technical side of the business through 2016.

I'm currently enjoying the next phase of my life...the empty NESTER! My husband and I spend our winters in Jupiter, Florida and our summers in Rochester, NY. We have three amazing children who have all gone off to carve out their places in the world, while I continue to craft stories that I hope will make you readers feel good and put a smile on your face.

Sign up for my Newsletter (https://dl.bookfunnel.com/ 6atcf7g1be) where I often give away free books before publication.

Join my private Facebook group (https://www.facebook.com/

groups/191706547909047/) where I post exclusive excerpts and discuss all things murder and love!

Never miss a new release. Follow me on Amazon:amazon.com/author/jentalty

And on Bookbub: bookbub.com/authors/jen-talty

Special Forces Operation Alpha

BURNING DESIRE

BURNING KISS

BURNING SKIES

BURNING LIES

BURNING HEART

BURNING BED

REMEMBER ME ALWAYS

The Brotherhood Protectors

ROUGH JUSTICE

ROUGH AROUND THE EDGES

ROUGH RIDE

ROUGH EDGE

ROUGH BEAUTY

The Twilight Crossing Series

THE BLIND DATE

SPRING FLING

SUMMER'S GONE

WINTER WEDDING

Witches and Werewolves

LADY SASS

ALL THAT SASS

Coming soon!

NEON SASS

PAINTING SASS

Boxsets

LOVE CHRISTMAS, MOVIES

UNFORGETABLE PASSION

UNFORGETABLE CHARMERS

A NIGHT SHE'LL REMEMBER

SWEET AND SASSY IN THE SNOW

SWEET AND SASSY PRINCE CHARMING

PROTECT AND DESIRE

SWEET AND SASSY BABY LOVE

CHRISTMAS AT MISTLETOE LODGE

THE PLAYERS: OVERCOMING THE ODDS

CHRISTMAS SHORTS

CHRISTMAS DREAMS

Novellas

NIGHTSHADE

A CHRISTMAS GETAWAY

TAKING A RISK

WHISPERS

Made in United States
Cleveland, OH
17 August 2025

19491564R00132